Madness
Of Love

A Madness of Kanaan Novella

I0540192

Karina Fabian

LASER COW
PRESS

Laser Cow Press

MERRITT ISLAND, FL

Laser Cow Press
Merritt Island, FL
https://fabianspace.com

Publisher's Note: This is a work of fiction. Names, characters,
places, and incidents are a product of the author's imagination. Locales and public names are sometimes used for atmospheric
purposes. Any resemblance to actual people, living or dead, or to
businesses, companies, events, institutions, or locales is completely
coincidental.

Cover art by 100Covers
Laser Cow Logo by Allen Oaks

Book Layout © 2017 BookDesignTemplates.com

Madness of Love/Karina Fabian -- 1st ed.
Print ISBN 978-1-956489-21-7

Dedication

To Virginia Lori Jennings: Because you wanted to
see Josh & Sachiko get married.

Contents

Chapter One

Sachiko's wedding kimono hung off the curtain rod in her dining area, where her Japanese grandmother had insisted she put it so she could ponder its beauty and meaning. A study of delicateness, the fabric of the dress shaded from a hint of pink at the shoulders to a rich but subdued rose at the skirt, the same shade of rose as the walls of the high-intensity ward at South Kingston Mental Health Center, the institution where she'd once worked. When she'd been dating Dr. Manipulator Malachai.

Just the memories she wanted on her wedding day.

The sheer kimono that lay over the dress didn't help. It was much too dainty, with the pastel flowers so sweetly and intricately stitched. It was made for mincing. Every flower, every shade, seemed to say, "Here is the gentle, submissive bride approaching her wedding with humility." To top it off, literally as well as figuratively, the white swath of the tsunokakushi headdress reminded her the good bride hides her independent nature.

Sachiko pointed her laser scalpel at it and imagined tracing a path across the tsunokakushi, down the piping at the collar and along the obi-jime cord—a stripe of satin more decorative than useful that made a pale highlight around the waist. One flick with her finger and the ensemble would go up in smoke.

Sobo could have gotten me the dress I wanted, the one I asked for. Instead she brought this. Submissive? Obedient? Does Sobo even know me, anymore?

Of course she does. She and Mama have long conversations about Joshua and me—even Nona and her talk about us and our much-too-long engagement. That's why the long lecture about tsunokakushi. Got to hide that independent streak.

Her grip tightened on the scalpel. She was thirty-four years old, long independent. A surgeon, for pity's sake. She would not play the demure and grateful prize bride, not for the press and not for her grandmother. Especially not for her amazing celebrity fiancé. Still, her finger hesitated over the button.

Joshua had bought the laser for her. "The top model for the soon-to-be top surgeon in the US," he'd said. It was an instrument of healing. He'd definitely try to stop her now, and it wouldn't even be about the dress.

Could she use his gift to destroy her wedding gown? Was she really going to be that angry—or that *independent*?

The doorbell rang. With a howl of frustration, she slammed the scalpel onto the table and stomped to her front door, snarling "What?" even as she yanked it open.

Papa stood in the hallway, giving her his loving, amused, and just a bit disapproving look. "Riqué called me. Your fiancé is in the hotel bar, playing piano."

She knew what that meant. Joshua always ran to the piano when he was upset. "That supposed to make me feel guilty?"

"He paid their regular player five hundred dollars to take the night off."

Great. She and Joshua have a fight, and some stranger gets a bonus and a break. She could just see him talking to his girlfriend: "Yeah, it's true! Joshaham from Chipotle gave me five C-notes and said to take the night off!" The hotel was probably having conniptions of joy over the famous musician playing sets in their bar.

Bet anything when he calms down, he'll send me roses, too. Meanwhile, I was about to slash through the wedding gift my grandmother brought all the way from Japan.

Forget it. I am not going to feel guilty!

"Well, we all have our coping mechanisms."

She let her papa in but didn't go back to the table. Instead, she went to the kitchen and pulled out the bottle of wine her matron of honor had bought her last week in anticipation of the stress to come "from the Japperwoppy invasion." Lizzie had gone through her own bottle in the days before her wedding, and she'd only had to deal with the Italian side of their family.

"Do you know what he did?" she asked as she handed Papa a glass.

His voice was calm but scolding. "Yes, and so do you. You know how your mama and sobo are. Do you think he stood a chance against those two?"

"I don't think he tried," she countered. "Mr. Oh-So-Good-With-Languages figured he understood enough of what they were telling him, he didn't think twice about what it would mean to me—"

"Sachina."

Why couldn't he bellow instead of that sweet little singsong of his pet name for her? Part of her wanted to scream like she was three, but somehow, that baby name reminded her she wasn't a child anymore. Besides, she'd already blown up at her mom and grandmother, and then at Joshua. Three tantrums in one day were too many.

She forced herself to take a cleansing breath and sip her wine slowly before saying anything more. "Okay. Fine. He got ambushed. Japanese is hard enough without two women jabbering it at him over the phone. But it's not fair to me, either."

Her father gazed at the dress with a gentle, wistful smile. He set down his glass and fingered the fabric of the tsunokakushi, the headdress that was part of the wedding kimono her sobo had so carefully carted across three flights and four airports. "Everyone thinks you will look beautiful in this."

Was she going to lose this argument with him, too? "Papa, I told Sobo what I wanted. I sent her pictures. How opposite can she get?"

He lifted a sleeve so they could see the pattern of flowers. Despite the heavy linen, the long, square sleeve looked like it should flutter instead of drape. "You know, it's a lot like the one she got you that summer we visited Okinawa. You loved that. You used to play wedding with your cousins, remember?"

"I remember tackling Masuto and forcing him to play the groom. Come on, Pops. I was six. I'm not a little girl now."

"No. You have been a strong, independent woman for many years now," he said with a half sigh.

Part of her understood. No matter what her age, she was his baby, and in two days he was giving her to another man. It didn't matter that she hadn't lived at home in over a decade or that he loved Joshua like a son. More than a son. They saw him as her knight even more than she did. Her family still said prayers of thanksgiving every Sunday over their having met. Her grandmother's statue of St. Jude, patron of lost causes, was starting to get a bald spot from all the times she'd kissed it in gratitude. The porcelain figurine grinned smugly at her in her memory.

Her temper flared. "Ah, yes, and such a miracle that a man like Joshua would want me. So quick! Dress in pink flowers and 'hide my horns of independence and jealousies.' Isn't that what the tsunokakushi is for?"

Her father shrugged, unaffected by her outburst, or at least refusing to engage. He had eschewed the mob side of his family to become a Navy Seal. Her uncles told tales of bar fights from their youth. Now, he was a married man and a restaurant owner, but he still had a temper to outmatch hers. Even so, he knew when she needed his calm.

He grinned at her. "Joshua said he'd wear one, too. He certainly has enough hair for it."

"Better than I do." She set her glass on the counter hard enough to make it click and tossed her hands in the air. "So, sure. Why not? We can both look ridiculous. The paparazzi will love that. Papa, can't you talk to mama?"

He dropped the fabric like it was red-hot. "Oh, no, bambina! I learned early on not to get between the women, not in the family I was born into, not in the one I married into, and not in the one I created. And now, your future husband knows that, too."

Her eyes narrowed. "And you made sure he knew, didn't you? Papa! He's going to be playing all night.

Probably lots of Chopin and Liszt, if he's past Rachmaninoff—or Pseudopolis, if he's really upset."

He shrugged. "Is that a bad thing? We could go listen."

The invitation tempted her: to sneak into some corner booth where Joshua wouldn't notice them and have a quiet drink with her papa while they listened to her future husband play. It'd be jazz or classical—complex stuff if he was trying to keep himself from thinking about their fight; smooth, easy stuff if he was settling his nerves. Chipotle might command the top ten in popular music, but he made magic with the piano.

She sighed. She had about four hours before she had to get to the hospital and prep for surgery. Chris—Dr. Prakash—expected it to take at least eight hours and had already told her he intended for her to perform a good share of it. It was a major step in her internship. She needed a clear head. "I can't. I have surgery tonight. I need a nap if I'm going to be sharp."

"My baby, the neurosurgeon. I could not be prouder." He crossed to the kitchen and enveloped her in a hug. She leaned into his shoulder.

"This is your day; you decide whether to wear the kimono or not. Mama will get over it. Either way, you will be the most beautiful bride of all time. Joshua is the lucky one here, and if he didn't already know it, I'd have made sure he knew that, too."

When he left, the desire to shred the tsunokakushi wasn't nearly as strong. Besides, half the point had been to exorcise her anger so she could get some sleep; Papa had taken care of that. She had one more thing she needed to do, however. She pulled out her phone and called the bar of the hotel where Josh and most of the wedding party were staying.

"Hi, this is Sachiko Luchese. I understand my fiancé, Joshua Lawson, has absconded with your piano?"

The waiter who answered the phone cried out in surprise. "You're engaged to Joshaham?"

She winced. Whatever possessed him to start using that as his stage name?

The waiter gushed about Joshua's performance. "I mean, I'm a big Chipotle fan. Big, but wow. I had no idea!"

"Yes, he's full of surprises that way," she cut off the waiter before he could continue fanboying. "Look, could you do me a favor? Could you get him a tall Diet Coke, lots of ice, a slice of lime and one of those little umbrellas? And then write on the napkin, 'She loves you'?"

"Absolutely! Is there a story behind the umbrella?"

Sitting a restaurant, hashing out some issue she couldn't even remember now but which had both of them on the edge of yelling. Toying with the paper umbrella because she didn't know how to say she was sorry. The silence stretching until he asked her if she planned on hiding behind her garnish all night. She passed it to him with her most beseeching look, and he'd smiled. "Apology accepted."

"Yeah, you could say that. How much do I owe you? I can give you my credit card number."

"You kidding? I've been looking for an excuse to get near him all night, and now I get to be a hero! What color umbrella?"

She glanced at her kimono and shuddered. "Red."

"Red it is. Hey, this is kind of romantic. Can I just say he's a lucky guy?"

The offhand comment that so closely echoed her father's made her eyes sting. She blinked before the tears could come.

"Not half as lucky as I am."

She hung up feeling better. Now, she could sleep peacefully and be fresh for surgery, her last duty before vacation.

Vacation! She snorted. *First thing on my vacation, I have to get my hair done and meet Josh at the TV station.*

She hated getting paraded in front of cameras, like she was some kind of hotshot just because her fiancé's band had recorded a few hit records, but that was the deal Chipotle's agent cut with the press to keep them from turning the wedding into a sideshow. She had a sudden vision of being Katniss from *Hunger Games*, told to be happy for the cameras.

"I'll be happy once this is all over and I'm Mrs. Sachiko Lawson," she told the kimono, and went to pick out a TV-suitable outfit before she took her nap. In a few hours, she'd be in her world, using the laser scalpel for its true purpose. She loved surgery, where everyone was calm, she was in control, and if she was lauded, it was for her own efforts.

Chapter Two

Dr. Prakash barely waited until the doors to the prep room had shut before rounding on Sachiko. "What the hell did you think you were doing?"

Sachiko clenched her jaw against her urge to scream Italian profanities at him. He was her mentor and would determine if she passed her internship, and like some doctors she'd known, he thought he was God.

Still. "I was saving that man's life. Isn't that why we're here?"

To give herself something to do other than strangle her superior, she stripped off her gloves and threw them in the biohazard bin. Any calm she'd hoped to find in the cool blue rooms of the OR had shattered as the surgery had worn on. Stuart Perrin's tumors had been far more extensive than the scans had shown, and his heart weaker than expected. Eight hours of surgery had stretched to eleven. Twice, he'd flatlined, and the second time, at 6:13 a.m., Dr. Prakash had tried to call Time of Death.

She'd bullied the staff to override his order. She'd had paddles in hand before someone jumped to assist. She'd expected Chris to throw her out of the ER, but he'd silently taken up his tools and began burning away at the last tumor once Stuart's heartbeat had been restored. He never let her participate after that.

Dr. Prakash leaned against the sink and crossed his arms. He looked far too clean and composed to have spent all night fighting for a man's life. Couldn't he have the decency to sweat at least?

"Yes, he's alive...and at what price? You saw the extent of the trauma to his brain. It wasn't just his heart giving out, and you should have realized that."

"He has seven kids! I was not going to go tell his wife we let him die and leave her alone with all those kids."

"No, instead you've very likely left her with seven kids and a vegetable for a husband. This was risky surgery, and with the trauma he's sustained, there's not much chance he'll ever come out of his coma. So instead of a clean tragedy she could cope with and move on from, she may be doomed to years of emotional and financial drain. She may come to regret that he survived this."

How could he say such a thing—and with that tone that said he was disappointed that she hadn't thought of it, too?

"Is that your concern? Or are you worried she'll blame you?"

He sneered. "Oh, no, *Doctor* Luchese. You were the one who took the extraordinary measures. You saved his life—for better or for worse. If she curses anyone's name later, it will be yours."

He pushed himself upright and with arrogant calm, removed his gloves and tossed them into the bin. "And now, Doctor, I suggest you wash your face and check that temper so we can go give the wife and children the news."

"Her name's Elise," Sachiko snarled. It was the only comeback she could think of. She turned on the cold water and splashed her face. Unlike Dr. Ice, her efforts of the night did show. This was going to be hard enough for Elise. She did not need to read in Sachiko's sweaty, frazzled face just how close they'd come to losing her husband.

"Yes, Doctor. I'm well aware of the family's names, and glad you are, too. Now, put on a smile. You're a hero."

That's how he painted her to Elise Perrin and her two oldest sons who'd sat all night in worried vigil.

"It's true," he enthused as the three enveloped Sachiko with hugs and tears. "The rest of us had given up, but she refused to let him die." Then he stepped back and with a nod, let her handle the rest of the story.

Disengaging herself from the triple-embrace, she took Elise's hands and directed her to sit. Peter and Joseph stood behind their mother, each gripping one of her shoulders. She wished Dr. Prakash had suggested his office, where the three could huddle together on the comfortable couch while she explained. Instead, Elise was left exposed, clinging to her sons' hands as she braced herself.

They could all see there was a dark cloud in the happy ending, and she ached at how strong the boys were trying to be. The oldest was something like seventeen. *Would he curse my name if his college fund goes to ICU bills?*

She couldn't think about that now. At least the waiting area was quiet and empty except for a nurse fiddling with a bouquet of roses while yawing her way through the last of the shift, and some guy pacing in the corner while talking on his cell phone.

She took a calming breath without letting it show.

"We're not out of the woods yet, Elise." As gently as she could, she explained the complications, the coma, the chances of his recovering either partially or fully.

Elise closed her eyes, digesting the information. When she opened them, she gave Sachiko a sad but hopeful smile. "We believe in miracles. You've given him that chance. Thank you. Can we see him?"

Sachiko watched as the duty nurse led them away, and as soon as they were down the hall and Chris had headed off to change, she slumped forward, pressing the heels of her hands against her eyes to push back tears of stress and exhaustion. Had she made room for a miracle or just set that poor family up for years of pain?

If she could, she'd just go home and sleep until the wedding.

She heard the squeak of rubber soles on the tile, and then a nurse tapped her arm. "Um, Dr. Luchese? I'm sorry, but it's just... There's a man who's been waiting for you for the past hour and a half..."

Sachiko looked up to see Gary, the personal assistant and Do-Fer for Chipotle, hang up his phone. He tapped his wrist at her and pointed at the TV. The news was showing someone's cell phone footage of her fiancé playing the hotel's piano, his dreadlocks bouncing as he poured all his emotions into the song. Even unaware, that man knew how to play to the cameras.

Cameras!

The interview!

"And here she is at last: the future Mrs. Joshaham— Sachiko Luchese!"

Mrs. Joshaham? Sachiko shoved her irritation into a corner of her mind and pasted on a smile. Gary handed her a rose. She'd snagged it from the bouquet Joshua had had sent to the hospital, and had the rest sent to Stuart's room. Joshua would understand. She only needed the one.

A nod from the stage director, and she strode onto the stage as hundreds of people applauded—some most likely because the digital prompter positioned out of view of the camera had told them to. Heaven knew there were plenty of fans who were not happy about the union. No one had told her *Mornings with Dan and Kelly* was going to be with a live audience today until Gary mentioned it as he hustled her into the waiting limo.

He'd foregone the seat belts in order to help her get her hair to do something other than look squashed from the surgical cap while he outlined the plan: They'd bumped the interview to the last segment and Joshua would keep them entertained with some exclusives about Chipotle's *It's Been Fun* tour until she arrived.

She and Gary had had to push through a crowd of screaming fangirls with protest signs.

Don't Do it, Joshaham!
Wait for me, Josh!
Trust <u>my</u> heart Joshaham.

They'd actually hissed and screeched as a policeman escorted her and Gary to the door. One spat at her and missed. At least no one tried anything violent. Most likely, they figured the marriage wouldn't last, and they'd have their chance with a rebounding Josha-ham in a couple of years.

Two minutes with the make-up crew, a quick change into her outfit, and there she was at last! The lucky fiancée of the hottest guy in America, the future *Mrs. Joshaham.*

Maybe psych ward pink was an appropriate color for my wedding kimono, after all.

Joshua nearly leaped from the couch to greet her. He wore a silk shirt unbuttoned partway to show off his chest, tight jeans Gary had probably picked out, and his hair in freshly coiffed dreadlocks, with her umbrella stuck in it. Had he explained that, or did they just blow it off as a quirk? He looked too young and wild to be marrying anyone, much less her.

His gaze caressed the rose, then her. He kissed her hands. The audience made appreciative noises without the direction of the prompter. They no doubt thought he was just a big romantic, but it was more than that. He'd recently started the habit of kissing her hands af-ter she came home from the hospital, his own little homage to the work she did.

She wished she could just press against his chest and close her eyes until she fell asleep, and then spend some time alone to talk to him quietly about why she'd been so upset. Instead, she took a seat on the couch be-side him. He settled comfortably with an arm draped across the back of the couch, but the cushions threat-ened to envelop her and his shoulder looked far too inviting. She perched closer to the edge with her feet planted primly on the floor. She probably looked like a prude. In fact, she could almost read the thoughts behind Kelly's vapid expression: *What could a hottie like Joshaham see in her?*

Casually, Joshua shifted position to better match her pose, lessening the disparity between their projected attitudes. No one would notice except maybe his parents, who'd trained him well in the use of body language. It made him a great communicator as well as an excellent celebrity.

And a great partner. She felt the tightness in her shoulders release.

"Tired?" he asked.

She nodded and apologized for being late.

Kelly, who usually took the lead in celebrity interviews, leaned forward enthusiastically, setting her hand on Joshua's arm as if to keep her balance while she focused on Sachiko.

"Don't even! You've been in surgery for the past *ten* hours, right? Operating on a man's *brain*? And we heard you had to resuscitate him. If it weren't for you, he would have died! What happened? Is he going to be all right?"

So that's what Gary was doing on the phone? Figures. He and I are going to have a conversation about confidentiality. Years of dealing with families as a nurse and now a doctor helped Sachiko keep professional neutrality. "There were some complications. At this point, time will tell. I really can't get into more details."

Joshua watched her with a besotted smile.

"Told you," he said to Kelly, probably referring to some part of the interview she never heard. "People make a big deal out of Chipotle's music, but this woman saves lives. What could be more amazing?"

Dr. Prakash's words came back to her. She told Josh in Japanese. "Stop. Please. I don't want to cry on television."

His brows knit for just a moment, then he held out his hand palm up for her to take.

"Oh, kiss! You know you want to," Kelly insisted. Her eyes shone with hunger for a vicarious thrill. The audience started to chant.

Now, her fiancé's face quirked for a different reason. "We made a promise when we set the wedding date," he started.

"Our next kiss is going to be as Husband and Wife," she finished his sentence. Whose stupid idea was that, anyway? She could so use a soul-engrossing, mind-blowing kiss from him right now. Nonetheless, she added, "It'll rank as one of the most romantic kisses of all time."

"Better than *Princess Bride*," he concluded, and again, the audience sighed.

"Tell us about the wedding." Kelly touched Joshua's knee to draw his attention back to her. "You're having Catholic and Shinto ceremonies, right?"

"The wedding Mass is first," Joshua told her. His gaze never left Sachiko. "I can't wait to see you in your dress," he told her, and for a moment, the audience was gone, and it was just the two of them.

"Well, we have a little surprise for you!" Kelly broke into the moment. "Most of our audience is not familiar with a Shinto ceremony, so we found one on tape and hoped you'd walk us through it. And Sachiko, we had a wedding kimono all picked out for you. Since you were busy *saving a life*—" She put a lilt in her voice reserved for talking to puppies. "—we don't have time for you to put it on, so we got Melanie Chu from Newport who was part of our audience today to model it."

More applause, and Melanie stepped out, wearing a red kimono with cranes and cherry blossoms. Sachiko felt her smile harden. Who had described her perfect kimono to them? But no, as Melanie held out her arms and did a slow spin to show off the sleeves, Sachiko could see the slight fades and snags in the stitching. Was her dream dress so common, after all?

Kelly interrupted her reverie. "Sachiko, would you explain if there's a significance to each item? For example, the headdress." She made a passable attempt at pronouncing "tsunokakushi" and asked, "Doesn't that mean 'horn hider'? What's that all about?"

Chapter Three

Gary held the limo door open for them. "I'm going to sit in the front with the driver, but you two behave. Remember *Princess Bride,*" he teased.

"Whose stupid idea was it to wait until the wedding to kiss?" Joshua asked as he buckled his seat belt. "I'm going crazy."

"Tell me about it." She put her seatbelt on loosely enough that she could slouch back against him. Kicking off her shoes, she rested her feet on the opposite seat. With the tinted windows hiding them from view, she had no problem indulging her sloppy side.

She pulled out her phone. On the screen, a count-down marked the time until the wedding. She added forty-five minutes for the Mass itself. "Fifty-two hours and thirty minutes. Thank heavens we have two re-hearsals, the dinner and the bachelor parties to keep us busy. Unless, of course, you were serious about the whole all-night vigil of prayer thing."

When he didn't reply, she tilted her head to see his face. He chewed on the side of his mouth, a sign that he wasn't sure he should answer. "Really? You were seri-ous? I thought you were making that up to get the press off your scent."

He shrugged. "You know I don't drink, and I'm not especially interested in roving from bar to bar...and there's only one woman I want to see strip. So, yeah, the whole Knight in Shining Armor thing kind of appeals."

"My cousins are going to be disappointed." She'd seen Vince and Jonny mapping out a bar crawl.

"Yeah, well, Riqué said he'd fix it with them. That's what a best man is for, right?"

She settled back against him. She felt so good and so right nestled in the crook of his shoulder. "I can't say I'm disappointed that you're not ogling pole dancers."

When what she said registered to her own ears, she sighed. She really did have horns.

"Do you mind that I'm going to party with the girls?" she asked.

"Of course not. You need to blow off some steam and relax. Planning a spa day before the wedding was a stroke of genius, too. I'm looking forward to a massage."

"Oh, me, too." She debated asking him to cut his hair, then decided against it. If she didn't want anyone dictating what she had on her head, how could she do the same to him? Besides, he looked gorgeous. It was just that she felt so mismatched sometimes.

Only in the shallow things, she chided herself. If only she could just disconnect that niggling self-conscious part of herself and bask in the miracle of their love. He was her soul mate, she had no doubts.

Slouching against him in the comfortable leather seats, with him rhythmically stoking her arm, she was starting to feel the tension leave her body for the first time in weeks. A nap sounded so good.

"Hmm?"

"What's the deal with the kimono and the tsunoka-kushi? Really, nobody really thinks you really have independence or jealousy issues."

Two really's in one sentence? He was such a lousy liar. Even after four years of knowing about it, he could not get rid of his "tell."

"Yes, they do—and I do have issues. I almost slapped Kelly Renault. She didn't take her hands off you the whole interview."

"Really? I didn't notice."

She snorted. "Every woman in the world is jealous of me, and more than a few would do something about it if given the chance. But it's not that, not *really*."

He paused a moment, considering her words. "Would it help if I told you I know that any meaning behind the tsunokakushi will last about as long as the ceremony?"

He pronounced the word perfectly. How many times had he heard Sobo say it this week?

He continued, "I mean, come on. I've met the women in your family. I have no illusions."

"I beg your pardon?"

He caught the dangerous yet playful tone in her voice, but chose to answer seriously. "Babe, you know I depend on that. I love how you take charge."

She sat up. "But that's just it! Look. We have a wedding planner who managed most of the logistics. My dad's taken over the food. Mama and Liz handled the guest list—except where your agent and your ex-girlfriend stuck their noses in. I cannot believe *Shank* is coming to our wedding. It's bad enough you're doing the instrumentals for his next album."

Joshua sighed. This had been an ongoing argument for the past two months. "LaTisha may be my ex, but she's also my future agent and Shank's current representation. This album is going to be a lot cleaner than his others. You know how I feel about that, and so does Lattie, which is why she wants me working with him. She thinks playing into the gansta rap cliché will hold him back in the long run. The genre's too limiting. He'll get bored and burn out unless someone leads him away from it. I don't like his lyrics, either, but they are imaginative, and the music is cutting edge. Besides, if Chipotle's breaking up, I need to expand my contacts."

"But a guest at our wedding? He called me a bitch the first time we met."

"He called you my *fiiine bitch*, and I took care of it, didn't I?"

She shrugged. She'd been about to slap that gold-toothed grin off the rapper's haughty face when Joshua stepped between them. *Sachiko is my fiancée and a lady, and you will never refer to her as if she were property again.* Shank had smirked and held up his hands in surrender, but before he walked away, he'd puckered his lips in Sachiko's direction.

"He's actually not a half-bad guy," Joshua said. "He just needs to be reminded of his manners."

"If he blows a kiss at me again or calls anyone in my family a *fiiine* anything, I'll remind him of his manners at the expense of his gold-grilled teeth."

Josh chuckled lightly. "He's been warned. My *fiiine* lady has a temper and black belts. Besides, I like him. I don't have a lot of family or friends. Meanwhile, your half of the guest list overflows one side of the church."

He put his arm around her shoulders, encouraging her to snuggle in a little closer, but she could sense the effort in the loving gesture. Had her papa warned him that he might have to go gentle with his tense bride-to-be, or had he figured it out for himself? It made her feel a little guilty—this was his wedding, too—but she couldn't keep her mouth from talking. He did ask, anyway. Maybe if she just voiced what was bugging her, she could be done with it and truly relax.

"My half of the guest list is taking a big chunk of your side of the church as well, and half the hotel. That's one logistics nightmare I am glad to be out of. Still, even that took choosing the church out of our hands. I picked out the colors and my wedding gown, and that's it. When I was growing up, I used to dream about planning every little detail of my wedding, and instead it's all been done for me."

"You're in the last leg of your internship, and we're having a celebrity Japanese-Italian wedding with a guest list spanning three continents, and only four months to plan it."

Some days, she hated that he could be so reasonable. Yet he'd been the one who pushed to get married when she had wanted to finish her internship first. "And whose idea was that?"

"You picked the date."

Because I thought you were going to break up with me, not to mention we'd been transported to a whole other planet, and then no sooner do we make up than I thought we were going to die...

Right after Christmas, Joshua had been ambushed on television with questions about the abortion she'd never had the guts to tell him about. The one she'd had while involved with Randall Malachai—Joshua's then-boss, another reason she'd chickened out. Regardless, the news hit hard, and learning that way—in public, from practically a stranger... It had played into every issue he had. She was sure she'd lost him.

Then he'd shown up in her apartment, dragged there by someone else she thought she'd never see again, a former patient, Deryl. Deryl had actually lived in one of those psych-pink rooms while the staff tried to cure him of his delusion that he was psychic. Not just psychic, but in contact with aliens. Only Joshua, the summer intern, took Deryl at his word—and it turned out to be true, all of it. With Joshua's help, he'd escaped and was living on another planet.

But he'd come back to enlist Joshua's and Sachiko's help. The neighboring planet was launching an armada, the two planets themselves were on collision course, and Deryl's wife was being compelled to psychically drain their world and most its inhabitants of their energy in order to push the other planet aside. Somehow, Deryl thought Josh and she could save them.

He'd found them in the middle of the fight—or rather, the long silence after the fight. The fight Sachiko had thought would be the last straw for her fiancé.

Who knows? It might have been. Funny how being told the fate of two worlds depended on you cooperating with your estranged fiancée.

"What are you thinking?" Joshua asked when she snorted.

"Do you think Deryl and Tasmae will come?"

Josh grunted. "They want to—Deryl told me when he brought us back. They'll move heaven and earth to do it—and if anyone can, it's them."

She laughed. In order to stop the planets from colliding, Tasmae had absorbed the energy of her planet to shove the other away—and Deryl had absorbed the energy of the *cosmos* to change their orbits with his brain. All that power, and yet, he's insisted they could not have succeeded without Josh and her.

Joshua seemed to be picking up her thoughts. "That was some adventure. You were so amazing—the way you saved Tasmae and Stormy—"

"Don't call her that. Her name is Hope, and you know it," Sachiko warned.

"If your Uncle Hiro can call you 'honeypot,' I can call my honorary godchild, 'Stormageddon.' I'm in the middle of singing your praises—don't change the subject. That was amazing enough but it was in your wheelhouse."

She snorted. Emergency surgery on an alien?

He ignored her. "But Salgoud told me how, when all the Kanaan were falling under Tasmae's compulsion, you pulled him out of it and forced him to stick with the plan."

"It was that or people died." In the past, Tasmae's people hadn't just pulled from the energy of the planet but sucked the life energy from its inhabitants in order to push the other world away. It wasn't until three humans came to their world that they even considered there could be an alternative. And then, they had had a hard time convincing them.

"They point is, Salgoud was in charge of their whole army. He's scary! And you didn't just stand up to him, but you made him turn his back on whatever siren spell Tasmae was putting out, not to mention five thousand years of tradition. Because you weren't going to let anyone die. That's just who you are."

His words made her think of Mr. Perrin, and it was like a fist in her heart.

She couldn't talk about that yet. They were discussing her issues about the wedding. Like they'd said when saving Tasmae's world, "one crisis at a time."

To draw him back to the topic, she said, as lightly as she could, "Just more evidence against wearing the tsunokakushi.

"If we were on Kanaan, it'd probably burst into flame as soon as it touched your head."

She smacked him, but the stress of the moment had lightened. She started to lean back against him. Instead, he pushed her away, turning so he could massage her shoulders. He hummed as he did so, and she immediately felt better. She may have saved Tasmae and Hope, But Joshua had discovered he had his own kind of healing talent, one that had nothing to do with drugs or surgical tools. He was still shy about it—it was the stuff of saints—but sometimes, he pulled on his abilities without thinking, like when he gave backrubs.

She relaxed under his touch, but she wasn't quite ready to stop talking. Besides, that's what had gotten them in trouble so many times in their relationship. So she steeled herself to continue.

"The thing is, I was actually looking forward to stressing over the details, doing all the prep work. But I held my tongue and let others take over because I am so ready to be Doctor Mrs. Sachiko Lawson. All I wanted was to pick my gowns. My kimono was supposed to be elegant and dramatic. I told Sobo that. I sent pictures. Instead she brings me a gown in a color I haven't worn since I was eight. So instead of looking exotic, I get to play princess in Psych Ward Pink."

Joshua's snort tickled her hair, but when she didn't return the laugh, he said, "You're serious? Like SK-Mental pink?"

"Put me in a padded cell. I'll blend right in."

He nuzzled her hair. "Sobo wouldn't know. Dusty rose is a popular color. Very Southwest."

"Well, they do live in southwestern Okinawa." Her joke fell flat spoken between clenched teeth.

Joshua shushed her. "You'll look amazing."

She sighed. Of course, he'd think that. "It's not what I wanted. Then she gave me a long lecture about the tsunokakushi and the proper attitude for a bride. It feels like everyone else is in charge of our wedding, but I'm the one who has to make the public gesture of submissiveness."

"Not if you don't want to. This wedding is for us. Wear your wedding gown to both ceremonies, or let's go get you the kimono you want right now."

She moaned. "No. I'd insult my family and hurt her feelings. I just..." She shook her head.

He snuggled her close, wrapping her in warmth and security. She tried not to think about how much she enjoyed the strength of his arms or the slight, spicy scent of his cologne. Fifty-some hours until *Princess Bride.*

"I get it: you're hands-on. That's what makes you a great surgeon. I took care of the only wedding detail that mattered to me when I proposed four years ago." As he gave her a squeeze, another small knot of anger in her heart untied itself. He was right. The marriage is what matters, not the ceremony. The kimono wasn't all that bad. Maybe she'd just forego the tsunokakushi. Her hair wouldn't work with it, anyway.

"You did take three months of concentrated shopping to find your wedding gown," he reminded her.

That had been fun. "I tried on probably a hundred and fifty before I found the perfect one." It was gorgeous, with exactly the right amount of lace on the bodice, and she loved the weight of the fabric on the skirt and how the folds shifted as she walked. She felt elegant and dramatic and absolutely beautiful in it.

"I can't wait to see it on you."

Then he whispered in her ear, "I can't wait to take it off you."

She could not turn her face toward him or they'd end up throwing their Wedding Kiss vow out the window, *Princess Bride* notwithstanding.

Fortunately, the window to the driver area rolled down, and Gary stuck his head in. "I don't know if you love birds have noticed, but we're not moving yet. Where do you want to go?"

Joshua pressed his cheek against her hair. "That's up to my lady. How about it? Want to go mess with the seating chart and stick Shank in the back of the room, or fold napkins or something?"

Sachiko sat up and stretched. She felt so much better. Even her energy reserves had started kicking in. That left only one thing weighing on her. "Would you mind if we dropped by the hospital?"

Chapter Four

"Why are you here?" Dr. Prakash scowled at her from the ICU nurse's station where he stood, scribbling notes on a chart. He wore the same suit he'd had on when he came into work yesterday, but you'd never know to look at him. The nurses sometimes joked that he had a pants press hidden in the basement.

"And good morning to you, Chris," Joshua replied with obviously feigned amicability. Sachiko had only known two people Joshua didn't like: her ex-boyfriend Dr. Randall Malachai, and Dr. Christopher Prakash. Unlike with Randall, who had been his boss for a while, Joshua didn't feel a need to pretend very hard with Chris.

Chris didn't even bother pretending. Without acknowledging Joshua, he said to Sachiko, "You are on vacation until June sixth so that you can do interviews and get married, go on a honeymoon, and quite possibly come back pregnant." He made it sound like an affront to his tutelage.

"We'll do our best," Joshua promised, causing Martin, the duty nurse, to snicker. He tried to cover it by pretending to sneeze and excused himself. Joshua gave him a wink.

Her chances of getting pregnant were probably worse than those of Stuart waking from his coma. Sachiko ignored them. "I just wanted to check on Mr.

Perrin, see how his recovery is going," she told her mentor.

He slammed his pen on the chart with such force that the pencils on the counter around it jumped. "Our patient's condition is unchanged. His prognosis is unchanged. If you are hoping for a miracle to assuage your guilt before your vacation, that's one wedding present you will not receive."

Before she could reply, he brushed past them.

"Someone needs a nap," Joshua muttered at his retreating back.

"He probably does," Sachiko retorted. "He was here even before me, and he hasn't left yet. He may not be the most diplomatic man in the world, but he's the best neurosurgeon in the United States."

"Not for long," Joshua squeezed her hand, but his eyes were keen with suspicion. "What'd he mean about assuaging your guilt?"

She glanced around to indicate that this was not the place for this conversation. "It's just Chris being Chris. It's fine. Why don't you wait here for a minute while I go check on my patient, and if his family's still here, maybe you could meet them? I know the older ones are big Chipotle fans."

Martin, who had been pretending to clean the coffee maker until Dr. Prakash left, returned to the desk. "When they left the room, she asked about the chapel. She was leaning hard on those boys. It's heartbreaking."

"Meet you there?" Sachiko asked Joshua, and he replied by kissing her hand. He might have questions for her later, but more likely, he'd learn it all from Elise

Perrin and find a way to help her through her worry. He'd have made such a great psychologist.

He's going to make such a great husband.

"You will make a terrible husband!" Sachiko's Uncle Hiro scolded Joshua from across the table at the rehearsal party. He slammed his hand on the table, making the silverware jump, but unlike earlier in the hospital, there was no real anger here, just some friendly ribbing of her fiancé. "How can you be a good husband when you can't even drink sake?"

Part of the Shinto ceremony was for the bride and groom to sip three times from a saucer of sake, but for the rehearsal, they'd used water. Uncle Hiro, who had had a few sakes at dinner himself, had decided that was as close to blasphemy as a *gaijin* groom could get. Never mind that she was American; he'd made it clear to Joshua that there were standards he'd better live up to for marrying into the Eto clan. Her cousins, even the ones on her father's side, were joining in, just for the sport of it.

Sandwiched between Uncle Hiro and her husband, Sachiko's mother picked at her dessert and pressed her lips together to keep from grinning. It gave a Mona Lisa smile to her perfect Japanese features. She'd look amazing in Sachiko's kimono. She was not going to join in the teasing, but that didn't mean she planned on stopping it, either.

Behind her, the quiet waters of the bay picked up the pinks and oranges of the setting sun. Tomorrow was going to be calm and clear, probably in the 80s. A perfect summer day for their wedding.

"Really?" Joshua challenged. "So you're saying every good husband knows how to handle his drink?"

"I think it's a survival thing," Joshua's friend, Leon, quipped and was promptly smacked by his own fiancée.

In the distance, Sachiko saw her Uncle Leoluca's yacht aglow with lanterns. She could almost hear the music. He'd offered his boat for the reception party, but Joshua hated the water. They'd managed to get him on a boat once, to film a music video, but the sea got choppy and when some of the water got in the electronics and zapped him through his synthesizer, he'd had a full-blown panic attack. She'd probably never get him on a boat again.

Still, Zio Leo suggested he have a party for the rest of the wedding guests, as a decoy. They'd quietly let it slip that the rehearsal dinner was there to draw out paparazzi who wouldn't respect their privacy. The seaside restaurant where they were celebrating was only too glad to keep the party private. One of her father's friends owned the restaurant, and it was Joshua's and her favorite place. They had been regulars even before Chipotle hit the charts. Many on the staff were friends.

No one had bothered with them, not for pictures or autographs. Meanwhile, Zio Leo had the reporters at bay. Two small boats patrolled the area around the yacht, and earlier that evening, she'd caught a glimpse of silver flying around the craft, only to plunge into the ocean a few moments later. Most likely a drone bearing a camera that her cousins shot down, literally or with an EMP pulse. Sometimes, the shadier side of her family was useful.

She would miss them. Once she finished her internship and Chipotle broke up, they were going to move to Joshua's family ranch in Colorado—far away from the ocean and her crazy, Japperwop family.

Provided, of course, her *gaijin* husband proved himself worthy of the Eto clan.

"I'll do fine at the ceremony!" Joshua protested, but Uncle Hiro just shook his head and waved his arms in dismissal.

"No, no. If you don't like it, you'll make a face. That's a bad omen—*bad* things for the marriage!"

Sachiko had never heard of such a curse, but of course everyone started insisting it was true. Even his parents were siding with Uncle Hiro. Under the table, Joshua squeezed her hand. He was enjoying the teasing almost as much as their family.

Their family. Wow. Five ethnicities, counting Riqué and Momarosa, and even more cultures. Their chatter wove a crazy quilt of accents in the cool night air. They had the outdoor dining area to themselves, which was probably a good thing, as noisy as they were being. Even her Japanese relatives had cut loose.

Beside her, her fiancé practically glowed. He'd grown up an only child with a handful of friends, but he'd always wanted a big family. He got one, an extended one at least. They'd agreed to give it a couple of years, and if she was established in her career but still hadn't conceived, they would adopt.

Maybe we could adopt from Russia or the Middle East just to add to the mix. She tried to imagine them in their own dining room, sitting at a table as long as the one they were at now, chattering in six languages as they rode herd on a passel of children. She couldn't see it; despite having a passel of cousins, she was an only child herself. She loved the excitement and noise of her big family, but it was a relief to go home to a quiet apartment.

Still, a couple of kids, maybe one with blonde hair and blue eyes?

Well, this was one issue she was glad to leave in God's hands. She definitely wanted children; together, they'd figure out how many. She hoped at least one would be theirs. Joshua would father the most beautiful children.

Kelly, one of their usual waitresses, tapped her shoulder and she handed her her empty plate without bothering to explain her starry-eyed expression.

As the wait staff cleared dishes and the volume rose, the predictions of doom got more outrageous, until Vince predicted ill for the honeymoon.

"Give me a break!" Joshua begged, though he was laughing as hard as the rest. "It'll be fine. I know how to perform."

The room exploded into catcalls.

"I mean, I can drink sake without wincing!" He tried and utterly failed to look stern.

Uncle Hiro poured him a glass, way more than was traditional. "Prove it. All of it, three sips."

Joshua cast a pleading look at his parents, who responded with amused shrugs. It wasn't like he'd never had a drink in his life, and his parents knew it. He just didn't like the taste.

With an exaggerated sigh, he picked up the glass. Treating Sachiko to a look that promised nothing but good for the honeymoon, he took one sip, then two, then three. Never breaking his gaze, he set the glass down.

Silence descended in the room.

Joshua grimaced. Not a lot, but just enough that her family would notice. She forced herself not to roll her eyes. He was such an actor!

"You see! Not good enough!" Uncle Hiro declared.

Liz, her maid of honor, threw up her hands. "Well, may as well call off the wedding. Now you won't have to wear that tsunokakushi."

Her sobo let out a squeal of protest and reached across the best man to smack Liz with a cloth napkin while scolding her in Japanese, which her cousin understood not at all.

Beside her, Sachiko's mom raised her elegant eyebrows in question. They hadn't discussed what she was going to wear—or not going to wear—for the ceremony, and Sachiko didn't want to discuss it. Better her sobo be surprised by the pink kimono at the ceremony. Maybe then, she wouldn't make a fuss over Sachiko not wearing the tsunokakushi. Either way, Sachiko didn't want to hear how proud Sobo was of her doing things properly, whether she wanted to or not.

She glanced at her phone. No messages from the hospital. Forty hours, thirty-five minutes until the wedding.

Now, Joshua was giving her the raised brows. She'd told the hospital to call her if there were any changes to Mr. Perrin's condition, but hadn't been able to keep from checking to see if she'd gotten a text. He'd caught her at it once or twice.

"Just checking the time. Wow! It's past nine, already. I think we ladies have an appointment to paint the town red, and my knight wanted to do his vigil."

"I cannot believe there's no bachelor party!" Cousin Jonny moaned. Still, the boys in her family seemed to be taking it with grace.

A lot of grace. A suspiciously lot of grace.

She got the feeling her fiancé might get his party whether *he* wanted it or not.

Chapter Five

Somehow, LaTisha convinced them to go to a little club she knew, with great entertainment—which, to Lattie, meant strippers. When Sachiko protested, she just laughed.

"Please! You think Joshua's going to feel threatened or something?"

Of course, he wouldn't. He'd have no reason to. Never mind that she was crazy in love with him, he liked working out, and it showed. By comparison, even the tan and ripped dancer in the stethoscope and a red Speedo couldn't compete.

Liz waved a twenty at him, trying to get him to come over for closer examination. Meanwhile, LaTisha had bought her way onstage with a C-note and was dirty dancing with a guy in half a policeman's costume while the girls squealed and cheered and raised their drinks.

Had Lattie ever danced with Joshua like that? Of course she had; they had been lovers. She doesn't even have inhibitions when sober. Bet if her sobo gave her a tsunokakushi, she'd wear it—and nothing else. Why is she at my wedding?

It was a rhetorical question. LaTisha had ripped his heart out before he and Sachiko had ever met. Even though he'd forgiven her, any spark between them was long snuffed. She was, however, a rising star in the world of agents, and when the band broke up, Josh would need an aggressive agent to build his solo career.

Besides, she's not a bad person. And I'm not jealous, even if she does have moves I can only dream of.

The cop dancer waved his handcuffs, and LaTisha caught them with her teeth while arching against him with a perfect camel move.

Sachiko knocked back her drink. She needed to catch up or find some good reason to get them out of there.

Beside her, Riqué's little sister was using her beer to half-shield her eyes from the spectacle on the stage.

"I shouldn't be here!" she yelled to be heard over the music and catcalls. Then she laughed. "Thank you so much for inviting me!"

Before Sachiko could reply, Sabrina held up her hand and pulled out her phone. She glanced at it and frowned with confusion. She started texting, party forgotten.

Before Sachiko could ask what was wrong, her own phone started buzzing. The sight of the hospital's number washed away the effects of the drinks she'd had. *Please, not Mr. Perrin! Anything else, but not Stuart.*

"I have to take this!" she shouted at her friends as she rose. The maître de, whom LaTisha had tipped with a twenty before slapping his butt, winked at Sachiko as he opened the door. In the cool air and relative quiet of city traffic, she called back.

"'Ko? Thank God this number worked," her future father-in-law said.

She looked at her phone to confirm the number he'd called. How'd he get this one? "James? I have my regular number off. This is for hospital emergencies only."

"I know, honey, but... Now, stay calm. Josh is going to be okay, but there's been an accident. You need to come to the emergency room."

By the time he'd given what few details he knew, the rest of the bachelorette party had stampeded from the club, phones in hand and horrified looks on their faces. They flowed around Sachiko, supporting her, helping her to the waiting limo.

Sabrina said, "I got your purse."

Lizzie clambered in beside Sachiko. "Is your gun in it? Because if so, I'm going to shoot my brother!"

Sachiko barely heard her. Her stomach hurt and her chest felt too tight to breathe. Sucker punched by life.

"I don't get it. I don't understand! Joshua hates the water. How did they get him on a boat? How could he have almost drowned?"

Across from them, LaTisha managed to look like she was lounging even though she was sharing the seat with five other ladies. She snorted. "What I want to know is how they got him drunk. Do you have any idea how many times I tried to get that man loose? Well, drunk. Loose was never an issue."

"Not helping!" Lizzie snapped. She wrapped Sachiko's hands in hers, but they trembled just as badly. "It's going to be okay. He didn't drown."

"He almost drowned!" Sachiko interrupted, while years of nursing and medical courses played scenarios in her head. "He's in danger of hypoxia, hypercapnia, acidosis, pulmonary edema, even neuro- neurological—"

A sob escaped her throat and she had a vision of her fiancé in ICU, tubes down his throat, needles in his perfect brown arms, machines recording the measured breaths of a man who would never wake.

I didn't mean it! When I said anything but Mr. Perrin getting worse, I didn't mean this!

Everyone squealed as the limo swayed into the other lane to pass a slower car.

"I should have married him already! I should have married him that summer he proposed. Why was I so stupid?"

"I've wondered that myself," LaTisha muttered and was shushed by the other ladies.

Fear and alcohol made Sachiko answer. "I just...I couldn't believe he wouldn't change his mind, you know? He can have any woman he wants. Why would he tie himself to an overworked med student who's a decade older than he is? And now..."

Her family was right. It was a miracle. No wonder her nona had kissed St. Jude bald.

LaTisha howled with annoyance. "We are not going there! Now look at me. Look at me! You are everything that man wants in a woman. You're driven and head-strong, beautiful and confident, brilliant enough to keep up with him in his interests and surpass him in yours. You're *everything* he wants in a woman, and I should know. I'm all that, too, and the way that man used to want me was epic."

What the—? As she gaped, mind reeling from grief to fury, the other ladies in the car started yelling.

LaTisha outshouted them all. "Shut up, bubble-heads. I'm not done!" She reached across and gripped Sachiko's arm. "You, Sachiko, aren't just everything he wants. You're what he *needs*. You're compassionate and moral and faithful. And don't even bring up the abortion. That Randall was a master manipulator. Trust me there, too. I know manipulators.

"The fact that you shouldered all the blame for so long annoys Joshua like hell, but he also admires you for it. That's the stuff that made him propose, and that's why he's stuck around for four years waiting. That man is going to be fine because in..." she paused to snatch Sachiko's phone from her hands. "...thirty-seven hours and fifteen minutes, he's going to marry you, and after four years of waiting, only death will stop him."

Liz sniffled. "Oh my God, that was beautiful! I'm so sorry I called you bimbo!" She leaned her head against Lattie's knee and sobbed.

"Stop it!" LaTisha scolded, though her voice cracked and her eyes flooded. "Get it together, girls. We have men to punish."

As her friends rallied, Sachiko leaned her head against the seat and started at the ceiling, trying to get control of her emotions. Thankfully, the limo's interior was camel rather than funeral black. That would have sent her over the edge. *James said he'd be okay. He's going to be okay. Oh, God, please. Let him be okay...*

By the time the limo got to the hospital entrance, everyone had their wits and their make-up back in order. Once out onto the sidewalk, Sachiko squared her shoulders. LaTisha and Liz took wingman positions at her sides, and with the rest trailing in loose formation, they stormed into the emergency room.

Disconsolate people filled every chair and lined the walls of the waiting room. Sachiko slowed to a halt. *What happened? Had there been some major accident or...*

Heads turned, and she realized half the room was filled with people they'd invited to their wedding.

The bachelor party swarmed her and started jabbering in three languages. Uncle Hiro shoved his abashed sons before her, forcing them into kneeling positions. "My fool sons took me too seriously."

"We're so sorry. We didn't think sake would be such bad luck for your *gaijin*!"

"It is if you spike it." Behind him, Shank snickered.

Sachiko's fists clenched. She wouldn't put it past the performer to have had more than just drink. If she demanded a drug test, could she expel him from her wedding?

"It's not their fault," her cousin Jonny countered. He was leaning against her cousin Ray, but she couldn't tell if he was intoxicated or too upset to stand.

Probably both; he shoved away from their cousin to fall at her feet, nearly topping Masuto and Mikio. He clasped her knees, sobbing. "It's my fault! The whole plank thing was my idea. I almost killed your future husband!"

"That's bullshit, Sachiko," Joshua's friend Carl grabbed Jonny by the shoulder and pulled him back. He had a bruise under his cheek and fury in his eyes. "We had everything under control until some idiot called the cops. Hate crimes? Do we look like racists?'

Sabrina and LaTisha had dragged Riqué to the corner and were laying into him in Spanish. He just kept shaking his head. He held a rosary in a death grip. Liz, meanwhile, had pulled her twin, Vince, aside and was giving him similar treatment in Italian, as was Lenny's fiancée to him in English. Two of her cousins were hissing warnings not to mention that their cousin Leo might have been at the party.

Sachiko pressed a hand to her forehead. Four languages buzzed in her head, getting more meaningless even as the volume rose. The duty nurse had started to rise from her station, and two cops were heading her way.

"All right!" Sachiko snapped, and for a miracle, the group around her shut up. "Liz, Sabrina. Basta! Enough! This is a hospital. Where's my fiancé?"

Riqué pointed at the secure doors. "That way. His parents are with him. 'Ko, I'm sorry. Oh, God, I'm so sorry!"

"Who's sober in this group?" she demanded. Riqué raised his hand partway, but from behind the crowd, Gary said, "That'd be me, honey."

They parted to let him through. His high-heeled sandals clacked on the tile. The gold sequins matched the eye shadow and glitter spray in his hair.

Sachiko's mouth opened and shut, but nothing came out. Helplessly, she waved her hands, palms up, at him. What other madness had the night brought?

He hitched the blanket a little more tightly around his neck. It only came to mid-thigh; the fishnet stockings were all that protected his legs against the air conditioning. "I jumped out of the cake, okay? It was all perfectly innocent."

"Innocent?" Carl snorted. "You offered him a lap dance!"

"He refused!"

"All right!" She was starting to wish the police would drag all of them to the drunk tank. "Look, Gary, just get everyone back to the hotel. James or I will call when we know what's going on."

"Absolutely! You can count on me. Oh, girlfriend, I'm so sorry. It was an accident." He opened his arms to envelop her in a hug, revealing a gold sequined showgirl outfit that fit him way too well.

She left Gary to corral everyone and get them to the hotel. At the security gate, she flashed her hospital ID. With a sympathetic smile, the guard let her through.

Inside, she snagged a spare doctor's jacket and a stethoscope from the nurse's office. She'd find Joshua more easily roaming around as Dr. Luchese and not the worried fiancée in a tight skirt. Besides, no one behind these doors had seen the fiasco in the waiting room, and she could use the aura of sanity the uniform gave her.

Her fears whispered to her with each step she took down the hall. James said he was going to be fine, she reminded herself, but another part whispered that Josh's father was a psychiatrist, not a physician.

It doesn't matter. I am a doctor, and I need to stay calm and professional, for James and Maggie as much as for Joshua.

Even so, she peeked through the curtains walling off her fiancé's area before actually going in. Joshua lay on the bed, head back against the pillows, but the bed was elevated to a reclining position. The hand bearing an IV loosely held his mother's. He had an oxygen mask over his face, and at that sight, relief hit Sachiko so hard that she had to step back from the curtains lest she cling to them to remain standing.

They didn't have to intubate. Oh, thank you, Lord. A sob tried to escape her throat and she forced it into a long slow breath, wiped under her eyes for stray tears, and pushed through the curtains.

Joshua brightened when he saw her. He pulled the mask down to his neck. "Hey! I get the hot doctor! Want to examine me?"

"Told you he'd be fine," his father's voice held more relief than annoyance.

Every family reacted to crisis in a different way. Joshua's tended toward quiet banter rather than tears or yelling. It was just another reason to love him.

She gave her future father-in-law a wry grin. "Well, at least he's a happy drunk. Babe, how much did you drink? And what happened to the prayerful vigil?"

He gave her a sloppy grin. "I got shanghaied. Riqué was in on it—my bestest man! And then your cousins said I had to practice, and then I lost track, and Gary was in a cake, and we got into the limo, and they put a bag on my head and tied me up and put me on trial for crimes against bachelorhood, and I wasn't repena- repentatent at all! And then it got weird."

He paused, and his brows knit in confusion.

"Do you remember what happened next?" If he didn't, it could be the near-drowning or the alcohol.

The chart, actually an iPad, hung on the edge of the bed. She pressed her ID against the face and called up his charts, checking temperature, oxygen, and blood alcohol levels.

"Are you looking at your email?" Joshua asked. "I sent you a note. I added something to our honeymoon list. Vince told me your wedding gown has a long zipper in the back."

His blood alcohol count was just shy of poisoning! Couldn't he do anything halfway? Was it too late to ask for Shanks' head on a platter as a wedding gift? Then again, she wouldn't put it past her cousins to have been involved in spiking his drinks, too.

"You're going to have the mother of all hangovers."

But his mind was elsewhere. "Unzipping that dress long and slow. My fingers brushing your skin…"

"Joshua," his father reproved. With a small jerk of his head, he reminded his son that his mother was sitting on the other side of his bed.

Joshua blinked at his mom as if just realizing she was there. "Hi, Mom! Don't mind me. I'm *really* drunk."

His mother produced a shaky smile. "Just concentrate on getting better so you can get out of here and take care of that list."

"You wouldn't say that if you saw the list!" Joshua burst out laughing. He buckled over guffawing until he started to wheeze. Sachiko opened her mouth to tell him to put on the mask, but his eyes bulged in an expression she knew from years of nursing. Fortunately, his father recognized it too. He managed to get a basin under Joshua just as he threw up.

From the other side of the bed, Maggie poured a cup of water for him to rinse his mouth. Her hands trembled so hard, she spilled some. Sachiko set down the iPad to aid her future mother-in-law.

She let Maggie help him rinse his mouth before setting a comforting hand on Maggie's wrist. Her muscles were tight under Sachiko's touch. *When was the last time she'd seen her baby like this, or had she ever? Joshua never mentioned being particularly sick.*

"It's just the alcohol, Maggie." She hoped she sounded more confident than she felt.

"Well," a voice drawled from behind her. "That and a bit more."

Another knot in Sachiko's stomach loosened at the sound of that voice. Jerry Lowder had worked emergency rooms in Louisiana and then Newport for over 30 years. Joshua couldn't be in better hands.

"Sachiko?" he exclaimed as she handed him the chart. "I haven't seen you since you left to work in that psych hospital. I heard you were moving to neurosurgery. What are you doing...?"

His voice trailed off as he took in the party dress under the lab coat. "Oh, no. Are you marrying this damn fool?"

"Guilty!" Joshua chimed in before she could explain that her fiancé was normally a teetotaler. "We are both guilty of first degree love with the intent of mononogary." He stopped to catch his breath and coughed.

"Put your mask back on," Jerry ordered even as Sachiko was snugging it back over him.

Josh winked at her as he said, "Monomalgy."

"Monogamy, and that's going to depend on if you can get to the church," she scolded.

He tried to sit up, but didn't even get his shoulders off the bed before he leaned back and moaned. "I didn't know the room really spun." The mask muffled his voice. "It's so weird."

"Just lay still and count your blessings," Jerry said. His fingers flew over the iPad as he accessed information. "You're the luckiest damn fool I've come across in thirty years. You've got a mild concussion from cracking your head against the... plank. Yep, a *plank*. That kept you from panicking when you hit the water."

"I was in the water." Joshua said it like he was just discovering that. "I was on a boat, and I fell in the water! I can't swim."

Sachiko and his mother both hushed him while Dr. Lowder kept talking.

"Not tied and bound like you were, you couldn't. Ironically, that pillowcase over your head made it harder to breathe the water in. You'd be in a lot worse shape, and we'd probably have had to stick you in ICU instead of in a private room for observation."

"Observation? What do you want to watch me do?"

Sachiko blinked. Could he be that drunk or was he just playing now? "Get better. We have a wedding."

"The wedding!" He pulled the mask off to make sure the doctor heard him. "I'm getting marry-ed. We're having a *Princess Bride* kiss. Four years I've waited for her. For Four. Four!"

Jerry raised a brow at her. He must be the only person on the East Coast—maybe all of America—who didn't know about their courtship. She shrugged and nodded, and when he answered, his voice softened.

"You can make it, if you rest and keep that mask on, and don't develop any complications. But if you're willing to wait that long for this woman, maybe you should consider giving up partying for her, too."

"I'll never get drunk again. No, no. Once is enough." Meekly, he settled the mask back over his face and lay back, shutting his eyes and breathing deeply.

"Once?"

"He doesn't drink," Sachiko told him. "He wasn't planning on drinking tonight. I don't even know the whole story yet, but my cousins were involved."

Jerry shook his head as he typed a couple of things into the chart. He knew her cousins. "Luckiest damn fool I ever saw."

Sachiko couldn't help but agree.

Chapter Six

With the excitement over and orders to rest, Joshua finally lay quietly while his mother took a towel and tried to blot water out of his dreadlocks. Her cousins had tied him up? She was going to kill them. The only question was should she do it before or after the wedding.

Joshua set a hand on his chest and hummed tunelessly. Or maybe it was a tune too complex for human understanding? Was he trying to heal himself? Maybe he was just drunk. Still, any little bit helped, right?

Joshua was nearly asleep by the time they were ready to transfer him to his room. A policeman intercepted Sachiko to see if she or his parents wanted to press charges. He seemed almost relieved when they said no.

It turned out Carl had had the right of it. The police were responding to a hate crime in progress. Someone had seen the shenanigans and thought a black man was being lynched in a racial crime. The police stormed the boat, catching everyone by surprise, and made them all hit the deck, letting go of the ropes that were keeping Joshua balanced on the platform. When one of the party members (Carl, she guessed, remembering the bruise) had jumped up to help him, an officer had tackled him. In the confusion, Joshua lost his balance.

"Two of his friends grabbed for the ropes, but it was too late. Someone dove in and pulled him up fast. The guy must have swum to shore afterwards. Do you know who that might be?" he asked her.

Leo. He'd been a lifeguard when he was a teen until he went into the "family business." Now he was laying low until some "family trouble" blew over. No wonder her cousins had said not to mention him.

What else could happen? She leaned against the wall, head back as she took some slow chi breaths. She shut her eyes, but she didn't have to pretend to be tired as she thought of some kind of not-lie to tell. She was so tired.

"I don't know who was at the party. They could have picked up stragglers for all I know. I'm just thankful somebody dove in, and so quickly. Otherwise..."

She had to stop. She would not follow that thought. She'd had too much alcohol and too little sleep to follow that thought. *Josh'll be fine. We'll laugh about this someday.*

At least her not-quite act convinced the officer. "Well, whoever he was, he's a hero. If you ever find out, do something good for him."

I just did. She nodded, eyes still shut, and listened to his steps recede down the hallway. It felt unbelievably good just to lean there against the wall, to let something support her for a moment.

"Sachiko?"

James' voice made her jump. Her eyes flew open. Had she nodded off?

"Let us take you home," he said.

Alone in her apartment with her thoughts for company and a pink kimono to remind her how close she came to losing the most incredible thing to ever grace her life?

"No. No, James. Thank you, but I'd rather stay." She held up her hospital badge like a shield. "I'll check in on Joshua, and I have some spare clothes in my locker. I can find a place to crash for a couple of hours."

"You know he'll probably sleep better than any of us?"

She loved the concern in his eyes. Joshua had that same look sometimes. "I know. I'll sleep better near him."

James's glance flickered to his wife who stood beside him, looking no more eager to leave than Sachiko. Only a few months ago, Maggie had been in the hospital herself, dying of a genetic disorder for which there was no cure. It had taken a miracle healing by Joshua and their extra-terrestrial friend to save her.

Deryl! He said they'd make it for the wedding. If he could bring Terry, he'd take care of Joshua in a flash. The near-drowning effects, anyway. Do they have hangovers on Kanaan? Would that be any harder to cure? You know what? Josh could keep that.

"Sachiko?"

She forced herself to move away from the wall. "Sorry. Mind was elsewhere. Listen, there's nothing you two can do here, and it's way past visiting hours. Go back to the hotel, get some sleep. Make sure my idiot cousins get some sleep. They're going to need it for when Pops finds out. I can't believe no one called him."

James' brows knit. "I called your house. I spoke with your Uncle Hiro."

She smiled. Uncle Hiro knew her father's temper. "It's fine. I'll call him tomorrow. Now, go back to the hotel and don't worry about us. This is exactly why you never have the bachelor party the night before the wedding. We've got thirty-five hours to get through this."

She held up her phone for them to see.

She accepted and returned their hugs, resisting the urge to lean against her future father-in-law. He was solid and warm. She rubbed her arms as she watched them go. Even with the fabric of the doctor's jacket, she was chilly. Her legs had goose bumps.

First, a change of clothes, and then some hot coffee. The cafeteria would be closed, so she might as well grab a cup from the nurse's station at ICU and check on Mr. Perrin.

As expected, her patient's status hadn't improved, but at least it hadn't worsened either, and ICU had a Keurig, so she got a good cup of coffee. Not that caffeine would help at this point. The only thing that could keep her up and going was a shot of adrenaline. She leaned against the elevator railing and watched with bleary eyes as the numbers climbed.

The nurse wasn't at her station. Probably doing rounds. A few quick taps on the computer gave her Josh's room number. It was a private room, of course. She frowned, resigning herself to sleeping in a chair. *I'll get real sleep when I get home tonight. Maybe, if Joshua's okay, I can get my massage this afternoon at least, and I'll sleep through that for sure. This night can't get any worse, can it?*

She tossed her empty cup into the trash can.

As she neared Joshua's room, she heard a female voice giggling and talking. She couldn't make out the words, but she knew that smitten fangirl tone way too well. She sped up her pace and pushed open the door.

The nurse sprang away from an unconscious Joshua.

"What the hell were you doing?"

Caught, flustered, and obviously trying to look like she wasn't holding a cell phone, the nurse nonetheless tried to bluff, "I'm sorry, but visitors aren't allowed..." Her voice trailed off as she took in the lab coat. "Doctor!"

"Give me the phone."

"I was just texting! I..." Her fingers slid over the screen as she spoke her protests.

Sachiko lunged forward and snagged it from her hands.

"Hey! You can't do that!"

Sachiko gave her a disdainful doctor look before giving her attention to the phone. She expected to find the photos deleted, any evidence of wrongdoing erased. Instead, she found the screen showing an upload menu for MyCelebSelfie.

Hands shaking with fury, she backed out of the menu. "How many have you uploaded?" She flipped through the photos. There was Nursie, her head on sleeping Joshua's shoulder. Her pretty blond hair, freed of any semblance of a professional, sanitary style, spilled around her face, framing it perfectly.

"None. It's not like that. I was making a private file. They were mementos. I'm such a fan. They were just for me."

Nursie pointing at sleeping Joshua, his gas mask still on, and she smiling like one of the puppies on her uniform had come to life and wanted to play. Sachiko's scowl deepened.

Madness of Love 🌐 55

"Which is why you were posting on an amateur paparazzi site. How many?"

"None! I swear. I was taking one more and I was going to upload the batch when you came in. What's the big deal, anyway? Do you know who this is? Joshua Abraham Lawson! Joshaham of Chipotle." The nurse flung back her head in exasperation, making her hair flip over her shoulder. She ran her fingers through it, letting it drop upon her back. Then she gave it a shake. She was as bad as some of the women in Chipotle's videos! *Was that her game—maybe they'll love my hair so much they'll put me in a video? People had done crazier things, but really!*

Nursie was still going on as if Joshua's fame was an excuse. "He's mega! He's gorgeous!"

"He's unconscious! Do you have any idea the ethics you've violated?"

Sachiko returned her attention to the phone. *Oh, look! There was one with Nursie kissing Joshua's gas mask!* Sachiko gripped the phone so hard the bling-encrusted casing creaked. "Who is your supervisor?"

"Oh, my God. Do we really have to bring him into this?" The nurse didn't plead, but rather whined as if Sachiko were being unreasonable. "If you knew anything about Joshua Lawson, you'd know he's always cool about getting photos with his fans. He'll probably think it's funny."

She could just imagine the horrified expression on her fiancé's face. "Patients don't just trust us with their health. They trust us to respect their privacy and treat them with dignity. Do you think this does any of that?"

She held up the photo of the nurse pretending to share Joshua's oxygen with him. At least she'd flopped her pretty mane to one side so he wasn't breathing her hair in.

When the nurse didn't reply, neither to protest nor apologize, Sachiko blacked out the screen and stuck the phone in her pocket. "I'll be keeping this until the morning. You can have it back after we've discussed your hobby with your supervisor."

She gaped. "That is so high school!"

"Then act like a trained professional and not a star-struck teenager!" Sachiko snapped. "Now, put your hair up and get back to work."

The nurse stormed past her, but once at the door, she apparently decided that as long as she was in hot water, she might as well set it to boiling. "And what are you doing here, anyway, *Doctor*? You're not the duty physician. What right do you have to be in Joshaham's room in the middle of the night?"

With fierce pleasure, Sachiko held up her left hand, the marquis diamond on her fourth finger having more clout now than her doctor's badge. "I have every right. I'm marrying him tomorrow afternoon."

The nurse's eyes widened. She might not have been fangirl enough to have recognized Sachiko's face, but at least she knew the pop star was marrying a local physician. She stammered an epithet of surprise but no apologies.

Sachiko thought she heard the nurse mutter "Cougar" as she left.

Sachiko clenched her fists against the desire to hurl something at the door. *Why does everything have to go crazy the day before my wedding?*

She stamped her foot so hard, her sole tingled.

Joshua stirred in his sleep.

Madness of Love ✺ 57

She looked at him, and her anger calmed. Even unconscious and waterlogged, he was still gorgeous. She couldn't blame the fem fen on that account. But why couldn't they exercise some restraint?

"For that matter, why couldn't you?" she asked her sleeping fiancé as she picked off one golden strand of hair off his shoulder. He didn't even stir. Well, at least he didn't wake for Nursie's photo shoot, and with any luck, he wouldn't hear about it until well after the wedding.

She pulled up the comfortable guest chair to the bed, and took his hand, her fingers automatically sliding to his wrist. She counted pulse beats like sheep until sleep overtook her.

Chapter Seven

A text alert jarred Sachiko from a nightmare, something about her mopping pier water out of Joshua's brain while Randall and Chris discussed her relationship issues. Groggy, head pounding, and eyes half-glued shut, she blindly reached into her back pocket for her phone and swiped the screen to see the text message.

I have ur $. Wher r pictures?

She blinked stupidly at the message until she realized she was holding the nurse's phone.

"Oh, you are so fired!" She rose to find the shift supervisor. Her head pounded and her stomach twisted in an ugly way, reminding her of the night she'd endured. She could not act the indignant doctor in her current state. A few minutes in the bathroom couldn't hurt, right?

Joshua slept quietly, breathing regularly, the mask hung on the hook beside his bed. Apparently, someone had determined he didn't need it anymore. She caressed one stray lock from his head—he was not going to be happy about the violence the night had done to his so-perfect hair—checked his chart to reassure herself that he was recovering, and sneaked into the bathroom.

The cool water felt good against her eyelids. She washed her face twice, once to remove the oils and make-up, a second time just to enjoy the lather. She used the complimentary toiletries kit. She'd get him another toothbrush when he woke up, and he didn't need the comb, anyway. Fortunately, her hair had adapted well to the new cut. Even long and full of product, it fell into reasonable shape. She nodded at her reflection. At least she looked better. Now, if she could just get five more minutes to attend to other matters, she could face this day.

Not a minute after sitting down on the toilet, she heard the door to the hospital room open and someone step in. She debated getting up, but discarded the idea. It was too early for visitors still, so whoever was there was doing a job. Besides, if it was Nursie, she wasn't going to find her phone, anyway. Sachiko gave a wicked grin at the mobile device sitting on the counter next to hers.

Her own phone started to vibrate.

She turned away from it, and pinched the bridge of her nose. *It was too early for the insanity to start. Come on! Can't I get just five minutes?*

As if in answer, she heard Joshua yelp.

Of course not. Sachiko started to rise, but her intestines gave a twist and her body demanded she sit down and tend to it first.

"What am I doing in the hospital?" Joshua demanded. "What day is it? *Did I miss my wedding?*"

The nurse—Nursie, in fact—shushed him. "You need to lay back down and rest. You've been through an ordeal. You have to think about yourself, Joshaham."

Joshaham? There are days I hate that he chose that for a stage name. Does Maggie cringe every time some besotted fangirl uses her pet name for her son? Sachiko pounded a fist against her knee.

"Babe, it's all right!" she hollered, but no one heard her. Joshua kept asking the same stupid questions and working himself into a panic while Nursie kept trying to calm him without bothering to answer the one question that would do the trick.

Her phone rang. The hospital.

She bit back a howl of frustration. What now? She took a deep breath to calm herself, and answered in a composed voice, as if she were in her quiet apartment and not in a hospital bathroom pulling up her pants while on the other side of the door, her fiancé coughed and apparently tried to get out of bed while a paparazzi nurse tried to coax him to lie back down and was probably enjoying laying her hands on him.

The hospital receptionist was a tiny island of sanity, with land mines. "Dr. Luchese? What's your location and availability?"

Joshua's coughs had turned to wheezes, and the nurse's voice was getting strained.

I'm in the middle of the worst day of my life with my pants unzipped, but hey, I'm available for more chaos! "I'm on vacation, but here in the hospital. I'm kind of occupied."

From the other room, Nursie said, "Joshaham, you have to calm down. You nearly drowned, you know."

Sachiko gasped. "No! Don't!" If one thing could make all this worse, it would be to tell him that, especially if he didn't remember.

"I did *what?* I was on a boat? I was in the... I fell in the..."

Sachiko swore.

"Doctor?" the receptionist asked.

"I have to go," she told the receptionist and hung up before she heard her reply. Making sure her blouse was tucked in and her fly zipped, she shoved both phones into the pockets of the lab coat and burst into the hospital room.

Joshua was sitting up in bed, sheets askew, breathing too fast and shallow to continue narrating his panic attack. He kept blocking the nurse as she frantically tried to get the oxygen mask on him. She probably thought he was having a relapse, but Joshua was smart enough to know he was hyperventilating, even if he was too hysterical to do much about it.

Sachiko didn't even bother to educate the nurse. Instead, she shoved past her and with a hand on each side of her fiancé's head, forced him to look at her. "Hey! Do you want to get married?"

A thin sheen of sweat coated his face, and his skin was cool. His eyes bulged so the whites looked unnaturally stark against his skin. But he nodded.

The nurse sputtered protests over her rough treatment. Over the hospital intercom, someone paged her. She ignored them both.

"Then get a hold of yourself. You're on dry land. The wedding's *tomorrow*. Now, breathe. You're a singer for pity's sake. You know how to control your breathing."

Again, Joshua nodded, and he cupped his hands over his mouth and nose, pressing one nostril closed while he fought to slow his breathing.

She could feel him shaking. She caressed his hair. It felt nasty from petroleum and sea water.

"There you go," she soothed. "We have thirty hours before we have to be at the church. You need to rest and to breathe..."

"Dr. Luchese, please report to ICU STAT."

She tried not to wince. Not now! She couldn't go. How could she leave him like this? She was on vacation. She didn't have to respond to calls.

She didn't want to know what waited in ICU.

But Joshua removed one hand from his face to wave her away. "Go!" he gasped out.

"I love you." She kissed his head, and the smell attacked her nostrils, making her grunt. "You smell like the pier."

Despite everything, he chuckled.

She almost ran into another nurse on her way out the door.

"What's going on in here?" he asked.

She answered in a professional staccato: "Our patient was hyperventilating. Keep him calm and instruct him to breathe. He knows what to do. This isn't his first panic attack."

"Hey!" Josh yelled in protest.

She bit back a smile of relief that he had the breath to do so. "Are you the supervising nurse? Then, when I get back from ICU, we need to talk about your subordinate's unprofessional behavior."

She pulled out the phone from her pocket, swiped it to reveal the text message and held it up for the supervisor to see. His brows knit in confusion. She flipped to a photo. The intercom paged her again just as comprehension and aghast washed over his features.

"When I get back. Don't leave," she told them both and took off.

Chris scowled at her from the ICU nurse's station, and as she approached, the duty nurse rose with mumbled excuses and left.

She didn't bother explaining why it took so long for her to report even though she'd been in the building the whole time. Chris wouldn't care, and might have had some sarcastic comeback like, "Next time, I'll ask our patients to wait, then." Besides, it didn't matter to the situation at hand. "What's the status?"

"Mr. Perrin has had a hemorrhage."

"Why did you page me to ICU then? Is the OR being prepped? We should—"

"We will do nothing, Doctor. It's time to let nature take its course."

"But it's a hemorrhage! We can treat that. We're talking about saving a man's life!"

"No," he countered, "we are prolonging a man's death. If he survives surgery, he will be no better off than he was this morning, and most likely worse. It's time to accept the inevitable, Doctor."

The calm in his voice made Sachiko want to scream. She concentrated on her fury. It kept her from bursting into tears in the middle of ICU.

"Then why did you even call me here? I'm on vacation, remember? Interviews, wedding, maybe come back pregnant?"

His only response to her throwing his earlier words back at him was to cross his arms. "The wedding is tomorrow. You are still in town. You asked to be apprised. What did I tell you when I took you as an intern?"

The question hit her like a hammer blow, all the more so because she knew exactly where he was going with it, and she knew he was right. "That being a neurosurgeon was the hardest and most rewarding form of medicine. That if you could, you would make sure I experienced it all as an intern, especially the hard parts, so I'd know what I was getting into."

He nodded. "There will be times in your career when a medical crisis coincides with family events, and you will be called to juggle them. There will be no balance. There will be no moments to regroup. You will have put your personal needs aside to deal with them as best you can and in the moment. I could have protected you this time, but I promised you I would not."

"And I told you I could handle it. And I can." She paused to take in a deep breath, in through the nose, out through the mouth. It came out as half-sigh, but it did calm her some. With a second breath, she expelled her irritation at Nurse Selfie. That, she could deal with later, anyway. The third breath released the guilt over leaving her fiancé in the middle of a panic attack. *Joshua's strong and savvy. He'll be fine.*

Centered, for the moment at least, she opened her eyes and regarded her superior. "I take it you're recommending Mr. Perrin be taken off life support?"

His lips quirked in a smile, the most approval he'd show under such grim circumstances. "I think it only delays the inevitable and puts a burden on the family. Do you want to review his charts before giving your recommendation?"

Her chest felt so tight, each heartbeat hurt. The crash cart in the corner seemed to accuse her: *You should have known better. There is a time for everyone.*

"Yes, please."

Madness of Love   ❁   65

Fortified by French Roast coffee from the Keurig, she pored through the charts. The brain bleed had been dramatic, but given the signs from the rest of the night, not unexpected. His EEGs showed a slide toward a persistent vegetative state that had started sometime after she'd last checked on him. If there was a miracle to be had, it would not come at the end of a scalpel.

Chris could be cold, but he wasn't cruel. He gave the Perrin boys money for milkshakes while he and Sachiko took their mother into his office. He directed her to the couch, Sachiko beside her, while he settled into the chair opposite. Taking her hands, he told her in gentle tones what the hemorrhage meant and what he and Sachiko believed would happen if her husband was kept on life support.

"The choice is yours," he concluded, "but there's not much hope."

"There's always hope," she replied, but it was an automatic response. She rubbed her thumb against her wedding ring and didn't look at either of them. "Is he suffering?"

"He's not aware of anything, not anymore."

She nodded, though Sachiko couldn't tell if Chris' answer made her decision easier or harder. "Before the surgery, he wanted to talk about this, and I wouldn't. I, I couldn't bear to think that... I can't. I don't know."

Sachiko wrapped an arm around her shoulder, bracing her. "You grew up together, right? You've been married for twenty-two years. You know. What would he have said?"

She sniffled, and straightened her fingers to see her ring. Rather than a diamond, she had a simple band with a cross etched into it. "Don't hold him back. Don't be afraid of what would happen to me and the kids. That he would be with God, and that I am stronger than I think I am. God would be with me—and he would, too. Always."

She clenched her fist, then clasped her other hand over it and brought both to her lips. They waited in silence as she prayed.

Finally, she made a quick sign of the cross and straightened up. "I'd like to go back to Boston, and bring the children to say goodbye. Can we do that? I mean, can we wait a day before we..." Her lips trembled. She'd probably gotten less sleep than Sachiko had. The shadows under her eyes made her look far older than her years.

"Tomorrow will be fine," Chris said, raising a brow at Sachiko.

Why couldn't he just slice my heart out with a laser scalpel? It'd hurt less. I love neurosurgery. I hate this.

Sachiko licked her suddenly dry lips. "Elise. One thing. I'm so, so sorry, but I won't be able to be with you tomorrow."

She blinked, the gasped in realization. "You're getting married!"

She wrapped Sachiko in a tight embrace.

Sachiko stayed to help her break the news to her sons, and then Chris told her to stay in the office to take care of the paperwork while he escorted the shaken trio to a hospital volunteer who could help them get back to Boston. As she sat in front of the computer, her hands trembled over the keyboard, and her vision blurred as she typed in the requests. What was worse—arranging for a man's death or escorting his widow-to-be?

I can't believe she apologized to me! "Put us out of your mind and enjoy your big day." *How is that going to happen now?*

Sachiko planted her elbows on the desk and dug the heels of her hands into her eyes. She was so tired.

Chapter Eight

Someone knocked on the door.

"Come in," she called, wiping her eyes of the tears that had started to form. She thought she had herself together by the time the door opened. A fresh-faced redhead in a beige business suit and impractical heels strode in.

"Dr. Luchese? I'm Rachel Dansk of Human Resources. I'd like to talk to you about Callye Michaels, Nurse Callye Michaels?"

Nursie's nametag came dredging to the forefront of Sachiko's memory. Her supervisor must have seen enough to decide this was past his pay grade. Either way, it was a welcome distraction. "Please, sit down. I'm glad to discuss this with you."

The clicking of her heels stabbed into Sachiko's head, reminding her that on top of everything else, she was a little hung over. Even though the screen was turned away from her guest's view, Sachiko turned it off.

Ms. Dansk set herself into the chair with grace and energy of someone who'd had a good night's sleep. "I must say, I'm surprised to hear that, considering the accusations she's made."

"I'm sorry. What?"

"Do you deny, then, that you stole her iPhone?"

That little–! Italian profanities threatened to erupt form her lips. Instead, she straightened her back and put on her most haughty air. "I *confiscated* her phone, which she was using to take inappropriate photos of an unconscious patient."

Dansk's nails flashed pink and gold as she waved her hand dismissively. "Your famous boyfriend. Yes, she told me about the unfortunate selfie. I realize you were upset about your boyfriend's reputation. However, it wasn't your place to take her property."

"*Fiancé*. And that's beside the point. I'd have reacted the same way had I caught her—or anyone—taking photos like that of a patient, no matter who it was."

The HR woman spoke to her as if to a child. "You should have brought your complaint to HR."

"In the middle of the night? Allowing her to have time to post or better yet *sell* those photos?" When Dansk scoffed, Sachiko whipped out the phone and showed her the message. "Ten seconds, Ms. Dansk. That's all it would take to upload and send a photo. Ten seconds, and it's splashed all over some checkout line ragmag.

"And you know what? Joshua might be embarrassed, but he'd get over it. Hell, it might even help him to have a little controversy. But when his lawyers unearth this–" She swiped until she got to the photo of Callye making a duck face while patting Joshua's cheek. "–then, the reputation of this hospital gets put in peril. We are a major medical center in an area where some of the most high-profile people in the United States either live or vacation. As I reminded *Nurse Michaels*, these people trust us to treat them with professionalism and respect. Ten seconds, Ms. Dansk, and we would have broken that trust.

"So you tell me: Should I have acted immediately to save this hospital a lawsuit and worse, or should I have waited six hours for you to do your hair and make-up and saunter into the office?"

"I understand you're upset, but you needn't take such an aggressive tone, Doctor." Ms. Dansk should have been looking at the phone, but instead she was staring up at Sachiko.

Sachiko hadn't realized she'd stood and was leaning over the desk, but no way was she backing down now. "Upset? You have the day I've had, and then talk to me about being upset. And as for aggression, trust me: This is me, being very calm and reasonable.

"Now, I had intended to take this issue up with her supervisor and let him handle the discipline, but since Nurse Michaels hasn't got enough sense to know when to cut her losses, I'll be very glad to return this phone to you after I've copied the information off of it. And I while I am off enjoying my honeymoon, I will have someone doing a search for any other high-profile patients that have been on her ward to see if any 'unfortunate selfies' have popped up in print or the internet. If I were you, I'd suggest you be proactive, do the same, and take action before I return."

Ms. Dansk's mouth dropped open for a moment. Then she cleared her throat, and held out a hand, palm up. "I'm afraid that's not satisfactory. I'd like that phone now, please."

"I'm afraid that's not up for debate. I'll have this at your desk by close of business. Now, if you'll excuse me, I have work to complete." Sachiko pocketed the phone and sat back down in front of the computer. She called up the screen to a blank document and started typing the conversation and the events of the night before.

Finally, the HR woman rose and click-clacked to the door. Sachiko monitored her progress out of the corner of her eye.

She paused, doorknob in her hand. "I'll have to speak to your supervisor about this."

"As shall I." Let her take that however she liked. Sachiko's fingers flew over the keyboard. She just wanted to be done with this so she could check on Josh.

Ms. Dansk cleared her throat and tried a different tactic. "Doctor... Sachiko. Nurse Michaels had a lapse in judgment. I agree, but she's young and a bit star struck. I understand it might be stressful dating such a popular celebrity as Joshaham."

"His name is Josh-*u-a*, and we're engaged. In twenty-eight hours, married. None of which negates the fact that the nurse you are still defending has put this institution in jeopardy of lawsuit, if not by my future husband then by the next celebrity that causes her to have a star-struck lapse in judgment. Now, good day."

The hospital doors didn't slam. Sachiko wondered if that bothered Ms. Dansk right then as much as it did her.

If she held onto that phone much longer, she might smash it just to let off some of her 'unnecessary aggression.' Instead, she used her phone to take photos of the photos, email, and Callye's MyCelebSelfie account, then used Chris' cable to download those photos to a private folder, password protected it, and sent it to herself. She'd deal with it after her honeymoon if Ms.

Dansk didn't have enough sense to take her threat seriously.

Slipping the phone into an envelope, she marked it Confidential, addressed it to Rachel Dansk of HR, and dropped it in interoffice mail on her way to the elevator.

It should have freed her. She should have been able to put it aside to deal with the next crisis in her prenuptials. Instead, she felt like she'd lost a battle. She was so glad she could not see her reflection in the brushed steel of the elevator walls.

Seriously, who goes to HR to confess taking selfies with helpless patients? Why did I have to run into the one nurse with such a skewed sense of reality? And how'd I end up with the one HR representative who would side with her?

"I'm sure it's stressful dating an attractive celebrity." Like I was having a snit fit because someone took a pic of my boyfriend. Oh, what if Chris does think I'm overreacting?

She wanted to smack her forehead against the wall. Instead, she straightened her posture and tensed and relaxed her muscles one group at a time, head to toe. It didn't help as much as she'd hoped. She'd tapped her reserves and then some.

I'm not a hysterical female; he's got to know that by now, right?.

That stupid, snide remark about my getting pregnant—and Josh playing right along. He knows full well we've got a snowball's chance in hell of that happening. I'd better call Chris, or I could come home not pregnant and not an intern. Provided I can even get my fiancé to the church... Give me enough energy to get through this day, please!

The elevator chimed for her floor, and she strode out.

Her father stood up from his seat in the waiting area.

"Pops? What are you doing here?"

"I've come to take you home, Sachina." He held out one arm as if to herd her back into the elevator.

She backed away with a disbelieving laugh. What, was she fifteen? "I need to check on Joshua!"

He maneuvered to block her without looking like he was trying to do so. "Your fiancé is embarrassed and worried about you. His parents are with him, and we all agree that you need to go home, have a good meal, and rest."

Oh, really? You've all decided this for me, too? She wanted to snark a scathing reply. She wanted to remind him she was thirty-four and a doctor.

But she couldn't. The nurses were watching while pretending to be looking at the computer screen, and the old woman by the coffee machine didn't even bother to act like she hadn't noticed them. In fact, when she caught Sachiko's eye, she tilted her head in a way that seemed to say, "Obey your father, now."

Any fight she had left her. She forced a smile. "Know what? I am hungry. Let's go home."

She steeled herself against the shakes as they returned to the elevator. She couldn't look at her papa or she might lose what control she had. He seemed to understand. They rode down, staring at the numbers counting down from twelve.

"Your uncle wants to know how you want it done," he said with a grim, Sicilian accent as they passed the eighth floor.

Her cousins. She'd almost forgotten what started the whole fiasco. "Would it be cliché or poetic if we took them to sea and made them walk the plank?"

"Depends on the shoes we put them in."

He managed to keep her giggling with gangster clichés and vows of *Revenge, Luchese-Style* for the short trip to her apartment complex and to her apartment. Once she crossed the threshold, however, her mother ran to her and wrapped her arms around her. "My baby!"

Sachiko burst into tears.

Chapter Nine

Sachiko woke to her mother's voice and gentle caress, and the smell of her father's cooking. She blinked at the orchid design of her pillowcase. When had she gone to bed?

"What time is it?" She yawned.

"Not quite eight, baby."

The light coming from her east window registered in her mind, and she sat up fast. "In the morning? My wedding day? But I had things to do!"

He mother shushed her. "You needed to sleep more. Now you will be a beautiful and rested bride. Even Joshua agreed that is better."

"I'll bet. He's got a list." She smirked, but didn't explain to her mother. "How is he? Has he been released?"

Her mother nodded from the closet, where she'd gone to pull out the outfit they'd bought for before the wedding today. "The doctor said he's never seen such a fast recovery, but he is at the hospital, still, waiting for you. And you have guests in the living room. Gideon and Tasmae?"

Deryl! Of course he'd be using his alias, but he came! No wonder Joshua had made a great recovery. "Is Terry with them, too?"

"Maybe with Joshua? The others are here with the baby. She is darling! *Kawaī!* Sobo may never let her go.

Shower, and we'll eat and get your fiancé before your hair appointment."

As if knowing she was being mentioned, Hope gurgled and giggled from the living room, causing Sachiko's grandmother to loudly profess her beauty.

Sachiko's mama held out the peacock-blue blouse with orchids along the neckline and short sleeves, and a matching cream-colored skirt with a kicky flare around the knees. Seeing it made Sachiko want to squeal with glee. Her wedding day! She kicked off the covers and snatched the outfit so fast, her mother laughed.

She'd always imagined that the day of her wedding, she'd take a long, hot shower, reflecting on her years as a bachelorette and dreaming of her life as a married woman. In reality, she hurried to wash her hair twice, gave her teeth enough of a brushing to make it through breakfast, and dashed into the living room with a smile as her only make-up.

Deryl leaned on the counter, talking to her dad and her Italian grandmother and snitching from the platter they filled with food. Her nona smacked his hand playfully. She loved having her cooking appreciated. Tasmae sat in Sachiko's favorite chair, nursing the baby while her mom and her sobo fussed over Hope's bare toes and full head of black hair.

Tasmae wore a forest green nursing blouse with cream embroidery on the neckline, with a matching skort. Earth clothes, yet Tasmae looked perfectly comfortable in them. She did notice that Tasmae had left her shoes by the door. Was she respecting Japanese tradition or just uncomfortable in the low heels?

Madness of Love   ☺   77

It was all so beautiful and peaceful and ordinary! No one would ever know that her apartment had just been invaded by an escaped lunatic, his extra-terrestrial wife and their psychic baby who was only alive because she had absorbed a phenomenal amount of cosmic energy.

And, God willing, nobody will find out. I have enough issues with this wedding without explaining that to my family. She cleared her throat. "Hey!"

"Hey!" Deryl bounded across the room to pull her into a big hug.

"Terry took care of Josh. They aren't sure about Perrin, but they did what they could," he whispered in answer to her unspoken question, then backed away to smile at her. "Promised I'd be here, didn't I?"

Tasmae turned her attention from her daughter to give Sachiko a smile and a nod.

"I'm so glad you guys made it," she told them as she stepped out of Deryl's embrace. "We weren't sure you'd get the invitation."

That was an understatement. How did you send a wedding invitation unknown light years across a galaxy, or into another dimension, for that matter? Did anyone know where Kanaan really was? She and Joshua had settled for sitting together, holding hands and thinking really hard to Deryl, giggling and feeling kind of stupid as they had. Thank heavens, it had worked.

Not to mention, Randall was still on the lookout for his wayward client, and had made sure the records still showed Deryl as a potentially dangerous lunatic. It was one thing to come on the sly to snatch her and Joshua to his new homeworld, but to attend a public wedding while he was still wanted as an escapee from mental institution? Even with awesome psychic abilities, he was taking a risk.

His rolled his eyes, picking up her thoughts. "How many times were you there for me? You think anything could keep me away?"

"Besides," Tasmae added, "someone wanted to thank you for saving our lives."

She disengaged Hope from her breast. The baby didn't protest but turned and held out her hands toward Sachiko, earning sighs of adoration.

Deryl led her over, his hand on her back. He was in a good mood. Normally, he avoided physical contact, since it made it harder to block out the thoughts of the other person. He used to be so standoffish and paranoid. It was so good to see him grow into a confident man.

Her father scolded her as he brought platters of food to the table. "Why didn't you ever tell us you saved a mother and child?"

"It was a team effort." Some kind of psychic attack had caused Tasmae's insides to *explode*, was the best way Sachiko could describe it now. She'd done her best to sew everything back together while a half-dozen alien healers used their psychic talent to keep Tasmae breathing and her body functioning while accelerating her healing. Baby Hope was barely four months in the womb; Sachiko hadn't expected her to live at all, and had chosen to save the mother rather than let both die.

She'd thought even with her best efforts, they'd lose both, but Deryl had stepped in, hopped up on the psychic power of the universe, and done some kind of godlike miracle. Hope went from fatally premature to small but healthy, and Tasmae healed right down to flawless skin. How could she have told her parents that? Even with said aliens in her living room, along with Deryl, who by now must be an expert at cover stories, she didn't think she could explain it.

Fortunately, her family brushed it off as Sachiko being modest, and Deryl, aka Gideon, played along. "Sachiko underestimates her part, as usual. If she hadn't been there, my beautiful women wouldn't have had a chance at all," he said, and Hope gurgled as if agreeing with her daddy.

"Maybe," Sachiko answered Deryl, "but you know I could not have saved them on my own."

"Nothing wrong with teamwork," Deryl admitted.

Once again, Hope held out healthy, chubby arms toward Sachiko.

"Ai!" Sobo squealed in protest and snagged a dishcloth off the table for a burping rag to protect Sachiko's outfit. From the kitchen, her nona protested that baby spit was good luck.

Sachiko pressed Hope against her chest, nuzzling her soft, thick hair and breathing in that baby scent that apparently spanned all humanoid species. Her eyes drifted to the kimono hanging on her curtain rod, the tsunokakushi draped carefully on the hanger with it. Maybe it wasn't so bad, after all.

They sat for breakfast, Hope cuddling in Sachiko's lap. Tasmae stuck to the fruits and vegetables, but Deryl heaped his plate. Her nona exclaimed her delight.

"Travel makes me hungry," he said, grinning at Sachiko. Teleporting across the galaxy did take a lot out of a guy.

The phone rang, but her papa waved for her to eat while he answered it.

"You know this is her wedding day, right?" He sighed, more of a half-growl, and passed the phone. "It's your mentor."

Chris didn't wait for her to say hello. "Come to ICU, STAT."

Sachiko bit back a sigh that would have matched her father's. "Is this another lesson?"

"Yes." Then, his voice changed, as if he were smiling one of his rare smiles. "I think you will enjoy this one."

From where he was bent over his plate, shoveling food into his mouth, Deryl winked at her.

The waiting room of ICU had a party atmosphere, with excited children and adults that were still hugging and laughing. In the center of them sat Joshua, a toddler drowsing in his lap and a little girl leaning on his arm as he sang to her. Terry sat on his other side. He saw Sachiko first, and tapped Joshua on the shoulder.

"Hey, gorgeous! You look better." Josh grinned at her.

"So do you." He appeared tired but otherwise healthy. She raised a brow in question, and he jerked his head toward Terry. The healer shrugged modestly.

Still, from their pleased expressions, she understood now that the two had made a secret visit to Stuart Perrin's room sometime in the night, probably with Deryl running interference by using his telepathy to ward off the nurses while Josh and Terry used their healing skills. She really wanted to ask what they'd done and how, but now wasn't the time.

Besides, something else caught her eye. "Your hair!"

Instead of the tangled dreads, his hair was now done in a conservative cut. It didn't exactly add years to his looks, but it did add maturity.

Joshua's grin turned wry. "Gary brought in a hairdresser. There was no saving those dreads. Besides, does it really matter what's on my head?"

Terry laughed. "You say that. Sachiko, look at the back."

Joshua had "JL ♡ SL" shaved into the back. She knew he'd just set the new wedding trend for at least five years.

"You are such an adolescent!" She laughed. She loved him so much!

From behind her, Chris spoke. "And yet you are marrying him, anyway."

"In five hours and thirty-seven minutes," Joshua replied to Chris but his gaze was on Sachiko, and it made her stomach flip in a happy way. "Go see what you need to see so we can get out of here and get ready for our celebrity Japanese-Italian wedding."

She followed Chris to Mr. Perrin's room and found him sitting up in bed, with his three-year-old daughter in his lap, and his wife perched on the bed beside him, still wiping tears and kissing the rosary tangled in her fingers. The respirator and other equipment sat silent and unneeded in a corner.

As Sachiko entered the room, the child declared, "I told my daddy to wake up, and he did!"

It was the best wedding gift ever.

Chapter Ten

Funny how despite all the craziness of the week before and her angst about the wedding being out of her hands, when it came down to the ceremony, none of that mattered. Everything—from the wedding march Joshua had composed to the vows they recited—everything was all about her and Joshua and the sacrament they were sharing.

Joshua's expression when he first saw her in her wedding gown was so full of joy and desire that it almost stopped her in her tracks. How had she deserved this blessing of a man? Why had she not been smart enough to marry him years ago? It didn't matter; they had the rest of their lives together.

Aside from the usual Corinthians reading about love being patient and kind, she didn't have strong feelings toward any particular readings for their wedding, so she'd left those to Joshua. Besides, it meant much more to him; he'd clung to his faith despite everything that had happened to him while she had let Randall draw her away from her beliefs.

She was finding her way back to the Church, but she still struggled with reconciling who she'd been with who she wanted to be now. How had Randall gotten such control over her, anyway? How could she have been so submissive?

Water under the bridge, she told herself sternly. Then, her words hit her, banishing the dark thoughts of her ex. She had to stifle a grin. Maybe she would refrain from using that particular idiom around her husband.

Josh caught her smirk and raised a brow. She leaned against his shoulder as her father took the podium for the first reading, from the book of Tobit. Now it was her turn to raise a brow. She didn't know this story.

Joshua whispered, "With the help of the archangel Raphael, Tobiah chases out the demon that was ruining Sarah's life."

"Knight in shining armor?" Of course, that would appeal to Joshua. Then again, did she really mind it, herself?

Josh's mouth quirked. "Well, Tobiah didn't have a sword, just fish liver."

A snort escaped her, and she covered her mouth to stifle the giggles that followed. From the audience, her mother and nona glared, but her father kept reading.

6You made Adam, and you made his wife Eve
to be his helper and support;
and from these two the human race has come.
You said, 'It is not good for the man to be alone;
let us make him a helper like himself.'
7Now, not with lust,
but with fidelity I take this kinswoman as my wife.
Send down your mercy on me and on her,
and grant that we may grow old together.
Bless us with children."
8They said together, "Amen, amen!"
9Then they went to bed for the night.

"Amen," she whispered. She did like having a knight on her side, fish livers or not.

During Communion, Chipotle sang their rendition of "Servant Song." Their harmonies blended with the words so that she had to squint her eyes against the swell of emotion that threatened to come out as tears. *Let me be your servant. Let me be as Christ to you. Pray that I may have the courage to let you be my servant too.*

That came so much easier to Joshua. She would need prayers, lots of them.

Joshua pressed her hand to his lips.

When they spoke their vows and placed the rings on each other's fingers, she knew in ways she'd never known before that this was the best decision she'd ever make.

"Since the invention of the kiss," went the *Princess Bride* line, "there have only been five kisses that were rated the most passionate, the most pure..."

When the priest declared them Husband and Wife, and Joshua's lips touched hers, their kiss blew all the others away.

After a controlled flurry of photos, with Gary expertly choreographing everyone's positions, her female relatives took hold of her to whisk her away to the hotel to prepare for the Shinto ceremony, while the men of her family did the same for Joshua. The photographer snapped photos of Joshua's pout as they loaded them into separate limos.

"Why is he so upset?" her mother asked. "He will see you soon."

Sachiko smiled but didn't answer. There was a zipper with his name on it. *Soon enough, love, but in the meantime...*

"Sobo," she asked in Japanese. "Will you help me with my tsunokakushi?"

Half an hour and much hair-fuzzing later, Sachiko stood in front of the mirror, amazed at what she saw. Rather than trying to force her still-too-short hair into the usual style for the boat-shaped tsunokakushi, her hairdresser took a more modern approach of a French twist, adding some of flowers from Sachiko's bridal bouquet. The birds of paradise she'd chosen because they were the first flowers Joshua had given her added a hint of drama and elegance. There was just enough orange in the flower pattern on the kimono to keep them from clashing.

Sachiko spread her arms and twisted to get a better look at the sleeves. When it was hanging off the curtain rod in her apartment, she hadn't noticed how the sheer fabric played with the light, every movement sent faint rainbows rippling along the folds. Even the color of the linen kimono and obi didn't seem psych ward pink so much as desert rose. With the traditional makeup expertly applied by her sobo, she looked gentle and humble—and foreign and exotic.

She threw her arms around her grandmother. "It's perfect."

Joshua had finished dressing first, and was waiting for them in the garden leading to the temple. He looked so cute and out of place in his kimono, with his toes wiggling uncomfortably in their geta, that she and her cousins paused at the door, giggling, until her sobo slapped them and made them go outside.

"If I tell you, you look adorable, will you smack me?" he asked as he crooked his elbow for her.

"'Adorable'? 'Adorable' is for stuffed toys and baby animals," she retorted with mock indignation.

"And anything you want to cuddle and cherish."

"Good answer." She jerked her chin up, preening just a little. She did feel lovely in the traditional make-up, though more like a porcelain doll than a teddy bear. "I can deal with 'adorable' for a while."

Joshua laid his hand over the one she'd placed on his arm. "Sorry, but you'll have to deal with it for the rest of our lives. So you decided to wear it?"

"I figured you'll see my horns enough in our marriage."

"Not going there," he said, making her laugh. The wedding coordinator motioned them, and they moved into position. Joshua took his hand off hers to wipe his brow with the inside of his kimono sleeve. She didn't blame him. Even her linen kimono, made for the summer, held heat like a furnace. She wondered what would have happened if she'd worn the heavy, red one she'd wanted. Her face paint probably would have melted off. "Don't worry. We'll be in the AC soon enough."

"Oh, this isn't heat," he said after the Shinto priest said his prayers over them and they processed to the temple. "I still have to drink sake without wincing. After the party, I'm not cherishing that tradition."

Nonetheless, he did it with grace and solemnity, and she thought she heard a quiet expelling of held breaths from at least half the wedding attendees.

After the ceremony came more photos. The photographer took her to the manicured lawn. "Can you run in this dress?"

"Without my shoes, sure. Why?"

"Barefoot would be awesome. I want you to run, slowly but very free, you know what I mean? Arms out and graceful. See, the flowers on this kimono are so *recherché*. I have this vision of them flying off, the petals fluttering behind you like the cherry blossoms. I think I can Photoshop it."

She had so much fun dashing and twirling in her bare feet and fluttering sleeves, she was almost late to her own reception.

At the wedding dinner, Joshua had sparkling grape juice for the toasts, and none of her cousins kidded him about it. Riqué's Best Man speech began with the call to "bring out the plank."

As the guests started laughing, several long boards were set before the head table, and then the bachelor party took their places on the planks, pleading guilty to the crime of high stupidity and involuntary groom endangerment. Even Shank joined in, and her Italian-American cousins begged her to forego *Revenge, Luchese-Style*.

She looked more like a princess than a pirate, but that didn't stop her from ordering them to walk the plank. Everyone cheered as they jumped off the boards.

It was a tradition for the bride to change her outfit several times during the reception, and Gary had insisted the bride and groom match. Before dessert, her mother and sobo collected her to change, while Joshua was directed to another room. He tried to take it in good humor, but she could see his ire.

"You'll get your turn," she promised as she kissed him lightly.

As she hung up the kimono and tsunokakushi, she felt her eyes sting, and not from the mask she'd put on to remove the last of the heavy make-up. The kimono hadn't turned out to be such a disaster after all. She already had plans to turn her wedding dress into a baptism gown if they had children, but she'd hang onto the kimono for their daughters.

As an offer only, however.

Nonetheless, her heart leaped with joy as she again donned her white wedding gown. She spread the skirt out before her, enjoying the feel of the silk around her legs. As Lizzie zipped her up, she had to hold back a smile at the thought of Joshua's list.

Then, it was back to the reception for more photos, cutting the cake and the tossing of the bouquet and garter. As Joshua pulled her garter off to throw to the bachelors, he let his fingers trail along her thigh. He was subtle enough that no one noticed, but she found her own patience growing thin. From the way he grinned at her, he knew exactly what he'd done, too.

"You are a cruel tease," she whispered while everyone cheered or moaned as Gary jumped up and down waving her garter over his head.

He put his arm around her and rested his head on her shoulder. "I've been going crazy since our wedding kiss. I think it's only fair. Four years."

His breath tickled her neck in a lovely way. "When are you going to let that go?"

"*After.*"

She would have kissed him with embarrassing passion had Shank and LaTisha not taken the stage.

Madness of Love ⊛ 89

"Yo! Listen up, Motherf—" His words cut off in a squeal of feedback as LaTisha smacked her hand over the microphone. She gave her singer a dirty look, and he took in his audience's shocked expressions.

"Excuse me. I mean, ladies and gentlemen. I have a song for our bride and groom on the day of their nuptials."

Her hot blood turned to ice water. "Joshua!" she hissed, but he just squeezed her waist, so she pasted a smile on her face and feigned happiness like Katniss.

Within a verse, however, the strained feeling morphed into surprise and then genuine delight as Shank sang *The Lady is a Bride*. At the end of the song, she was clapping with everyone else.

"Did you know?" she had to raise her voice for Joshua to hear her over the cheers.

"No! But didn't I tell you?" Joshua stuck his fingers in his mouth to whistle.

That opened the way for music and dancing. With several professional musicians rounding out the guest list, Shank's wasn't the only original song written in their honor. Riqué grumbled that he'd been cheated out of the first spot, but his was the first they danced to. During another dance, Gary ran up to them and grabbed their shoulders. He pointed toward the door. He'd double-wrapped her garter around his wrist to wear it like a bracelet. "Tell me who that, that vision, is!"

Sachiko did a double take. She hadn't seen Deryl or Tasmae after the church, and had assumed they'd teleported back to Kanaan. Now, Tasmae stood in the entrance, looking self-assured if a bit befuddled. Her alien features were just off enough to not hold to standard beauty, but with her makeup, she looked strikingly exotic. Sachiko hadn't known Kanaans used make-up. Her ebony hair was swept up in an elaborate hairdo held by bronze hairpieces that matched a dress that complemented her bodybuilder figure. Her strappy sandals didn't have a heel, but with her height, she didn't need any. Gary wasn't the only man in the room whose attention she'd caught.

"Whoa," Joshua breathed, then cleared his throat. Sachiko forgave him; he looked as much shocked as admiring.

"I think I've gone straight," Gary declared.

Joshua blinked as if he wasn't sure he was seeing what he thought he was seeing. Sachiko poked him, and he turned his attention to their friend. "Sorry, dude. She's married."

"Any chance I could break it up, even temporarily?"

Deryl walked up to Tasmae and handed her a drink. They kissed.

Gary sighed. "He's gorgeous, too. I don't stand a chance with either of them, do I?"

"Very happily married," Joshua affirmed. "With a baby. Where's Stormageddon, Infant Princess *Commandante* of the Universe, anyway?"

"If we have children, you are not calling them things like that," she said as she led him to the couple.

"No promises, Babe."

"We took *Hope* home," Deryl answered Joshua's question when they went to greet them. "She was getting cranky and hard to control." He tapped his head.

"Good call," Sachiko said. She'd seen enough babies in a meltdown to know that Earth was not ready for a cranky baby with telekinetic abilities, particularly one who had absorbed enough energy on the first day of her life to power a star. Sachiko might chide Joshua on his choice of nickname, but Stormageddon wasn't exactly inaccurate, either.

"And Terry?"

"Terry was tired, too, but he enjoyed the ceremony."

"Now you're free to enjoy yourselves!" Gary muscled into the conversation. "But, girl, you have got to tell me who designed that dress."

Deryl popped off the name of a designer that made Gary squeal—and for Gary, who knew the fashion industry bottom to top, to show that kind of crazed fandom, the designer had to be on top.

Deryl twitched his shoulder as if it were nothing. "I don't get to spoil my woman much...or dance with her. So if you'll excuse us."

Without waiting for an answer, he took Tasmae by the hand and led her to the dance floor.

"Sounds good to me," Joshua said, then his voice took on a sexy purr. "I have not held you enough."

Gary broke the moment by shouting, "Take me, then!" and holding his arms wide in Joshua's direction. Joshua grabbed him by the shoulders and spun him in the direction of the bridesmaids. Then, he took Sachiko's hand and headed to the dance floor.

Her sobo intercepted them to declare it was time for a costume change.

Joshua stepped just a bit between her and her grandmother and bowed low. He said in Japanese, "Honored Grandmother, it is my turn. It's my right and my privilege as her husband."

"Ai!" She laughed and scolded. "You bring her back down here. We want to see her in her party dress."

"I promise," he said, but there was something suspiciously neutral about the way he said it.

He led her out of the ballroom.

"They expect us back soon," she told him once they were out in the hall.

"I know," he said, though he didn't sound like he especially cared what anyone else expected. His hand hovered over the small of her back, fingers toying with the hook that kept the train of her gown up and out of the way.

In the elevator, he gave her one gentle kiss. "I love you, Mrs. Lawson."

"And I love you, Mr. Luchese." When Joshua's band—and hence his name—had become popular, they'd decided that they'd use her last name on things like phones and utilities in order to keep their home life more private.

"Mr. Luchese, husband of the great neurosurgeon, Doctor Sachiko Luchese. I like it." He grinned and leaned down to kiss her again, but the doors opened on their floor.

She took the lead to their room. She didn't pause to let him carry her over the threshold. They were just there to change and get back. Or so she told herself, but she couldn't look at him. She faced the closet and reached for her party dress. "There's a hook above the zipper."

"I know." His voice was a strong, confident purr. His hands brushed her skin in that same cruel, wonderful tease he'd used when removing her garter, but when he undid the zipper...

He'd touched her many times in their four years together, but never like this, never with such intent.

Madness of Love 🌐 93

Her hands dropped away from her party dress.

"I love you so much." He kissed her neck as his hands caressed her bare back, brushed along her sides.

She closed her eyes, falling into the sensation. Other women could have all the photos of his gorgeous face they wanted. Let them enjoy his voice. But his touch. Oh, his touch!

She'd noticed it the first time she'd seen him play his keyboard, so gentle and strong and skilled. She'd dreamed of those hands playing upon her skin with the same passion. Did other women notice his hands and fantasize, too? It didn't matter; his touch was for her alone.

He slipped her dress off her shoulders as his lips caressed her hairline. "For four years, I've longed for this moment."

She still remembered the electricity when he'd helped her off her kitchen counter and into his embrace the night they'd first kissed. They'd gone through so much together in those years, and they had so much more to experience together.

Finally, together. As One.

"Me, too!" She spun in his arms and kissed him.

They lay in bed, holding hands and smiling at the ceiling.

"That was intense!" Joshua said when he could catch his breath.

"Tell me about it! I didn't even get my shoes off." She laughed as she stretched out one leg, still adorned in its sheer stocking and white high heel.

"I know!"

That sexy, enthusiastic tone made her want to pull off the shoes and snuggle against him. But they had guests waiting downstairs. She sat up with a moan of regret and pulled her gown against her. "We have to get back downstairs, and I have to look amazing for every-one."

"You do look amazing."

"In my party dress!" She felt her face burning.

Joshua noticed, and his expression softened. "I don't think I've ever made you blush before."

"Well, you've certainly made me self-conscious." The frank admiration and charm with which he looked at her wasn't helping. How could she want to jump him and hide in the bathroom at the same time? "What? Are you just going to lay there and watch me dress?"

"Yeah. It's on my list." He propped himself up on his elbows. "You can watch me next."

Now, her face really stung! "Is that on your list, too? You've got a kinky side, Mister."

"That a problem?"

She did not have a good answer for that, so she turned her attention back to the closet and tried to ig-nore what his gaze did to her. Was her back as red as her face?

Josh's phone rang. He sighed as he answered. "Yep? Well, what do you think we were doing?"

She heard Gary squeal over the phone and smacked her forehead. That kind of embarrassment she did not enjoy. She sped up her dressing and fervently hoped he was calling from the lobby and not where everyone would hear.

Joshua, however, took it in stride. "A few more minutes. Sachiko's going to wow everyone in her party dress. What?"

His voice took on a serious tone. She turned to look at Joshua. His mouth was pursed in a tight frown and he was reaching for his underwear. "How'd he get in? Seriously? All right, just tell them to hang on a few minutes...and if Gideon's around... Well, okay then."

He tossed the phone on the bed. "It seems your ex-boyfriend has crashed our reception."

Sachiko's mouth fell open. "Randall?" Without thinking, she pulled the hanger holding his next outfit off the coat rack and tossed it on the bed.

"Thanks. Yep. Seems Dr. Malachai is convinced that we have an escaped lunatic on our guest list," he said as he pulled on the pants.

Deryl. Of course, he'd know Deryl would come to the. After all, he brought us together. "Has someone warned Deryl?"

"Gary said he hasn't seen 'Gideon' or Tasmae in a while, but you know what a concerned citizen Malachai is. He brought the police with him and is insisting they search the ballroom, and it's making some of your cousins nervous."

Leo. Sachiko threw up her hands. "Just give me two minutes."

Joshua reached under the bed where his shoe had fallen and pulled it on. "No. You will stay here and take your time and come down looking amazing. I'll handle Malachai and the police."

"But it won't take me long."

"I know, but that's not the point." He reached into the closet, but instead of grabbing his shirt that she'd chosen to go with her dress, he draped the tsunokaku-shi under his hand. "Do you know what this means to me? It means you trust me to handle the family crisis once in a while."

Family. She kind of liked how he said that.

He let the fabric slide from his grasp and took her shoulders. "Let me do this for us. Meanwhile, you take your time and come down looking so amazing everyone will forget Dolfus Randall Malachai's intrusion."

Chipotle's song came back to her: *Pray that I may have the courage to let you be my servant, too.*

"Will you send Liz up to help me?"

He kissed her forehead. "As you wish."

He donned his shirt quickly, then paused at the door. "Text me from the lobby. I want to play 'Hot Romance by Moonlight' as you make your grand entrance."

Then he was gone.

She leaned against the wall a moment, feeling cuddled and cherished and completely at peace. It wouldn't last, she knew, but there would be other such moments, and she'd savor them all. In the meantime...

She pushed herself off the wall and finished getting dressed. She could submit to her husband's wishes in this. After all, he deserved it.

Please Leave a Review

Please take a few minutes to leave a review. It only takes 20 words to share with others what you like and don't like about the book. It helps readers and helps with Amazon ratings which makes author and dragon happy.

Subscribe to My Newsletter

If you want to keep up with my adventures, books, and classes in person and on print, sign up for my newsletter. You'll get a free ebook with a story about Deryl before the asylum!

https://fabianspace.substack.com/subscribe

Acknowledgements

Many thanks to my editor, Michelle Buckman, for making me go over the entire story, adding relevant details. It forced me to stretch my imagination and my skills, and in the process, I discovered some really fun things about Sachiko and her kimono. Special thanks, too, to Virginia Jennings who asked for this story. I'd long had the idea of the disastrous bachelor party, but never imagined the wedding itself until she asked. Finally, thanks to Ann Lewis. When the story refused to come together, she suggested I might be telling it from the wrong POV. I had been telling it through Joshua. Switching it to Sachiko not only made for a stronger story but also gave me the chance to get to know her more deeply.

There's More Fun in FabianSpace!

Thank you for buying this book. If you enjoyed it, click to see the others in this series or discover one of the other worlds of FabianSpace.

Science Fiction
Space Traipse: Hold My Beer: Redneck ingenuity and common sense in a Star Trek-ish universe. Enjoy the adventures of the HMB Impulsive.

The Rescue Sisters: Intrepid women doing dangerous missions in space for the love of God and humankind.

The Old Man and the Void: Dex is a relic hunter on the edge of the black hole, desperate for the catch of a lifetime.

Jovian Heat: As the next Great Storm of Jupiter rises, Cass must find the father of a baby in peril—but the father died before the child was conceived.

Fantasy
DragonEye: Vern's a snarky dragon on the wrong side of the Interdimensional Gap, solving crimes, battling evil, and saving the universes on an all-too-regular basis.

Madness of Kanaan: Deryl isn't crazy; he's psychic, and aliens of two worlds thinks he can save them. Maybe he can—but can he regain his sanity in the process?

Horror
Neeta Lyffe, Zombie Exterminator: Neeta's an average exterminator, taking out bugs, rodents, and the undead. Can she keep her friends alive, pay her bills, and find romance?

Frightliner and Other Tales of the Supernatural (with Colleen Drippé): Truck-driving vampires terrorizing the road, Southern women doing what needs doing, a zombie wedding—a great story collection for horror lovers.